To Prove a Villain

The Shakespeare Murders, Vol. 3

John Paulits

A Wings ePress, Inc.

Mystery

Wings ePress, Inc.

Edited by: Jeanne Smith
Copy Edited by: Christie Kraemer
Executive Editor: Jeanne Smith
Cover Artist: Trisha FitzGerald-Jung
Photo of man by Gabriela Cheloni from Pexels

Wings ePress Books
www.wingsepress.com

Copyright © 2021 by: John Paulits
ISBN-13: 978-1-61309-535-5

Published In the United States Of America

Wings ePress Inc.
3000 N. Rock Road
Newton, KS 67114

Dedication

To all of the good people at Giando on the Water

One

The season ended. The final word of the final performance of Chekhov's *The Seagull* had been spoken. The final member of the final audience filed out of the theater. Good-byes, member to member of the AWB Theatre Company circulated through the ranks, and the Bouwerie Lane Theatre sank into idleness. Mark Louis, actor and newly appointed managing director of the theater, promised to let the other actors know by July fifteenth, two months hence, whether they would get a jump on next season by putting on some Shakespeare in late August. Since the theater had to start raising its own money and paying its own keep, they would have to offer shows more frequently.

Now, two weeks into the vacation on the first morning in June, Mark lay in bed in his dismal Avenue B one-room apartment. Somehow, even with the din of downtown outside his open window, it seemed too quiet. He had nothing to do. He hadn't realized how much the tension of making the theater a success had been a part of him. He promised Kristy King, his acting company colleague and mostly live-in lover, he'd spend these two summer months doing some writing, but with so little success, merely a few published short stories, albeit in reputable mystery magazines, his motivation to write had waned. He started another novel, his third, as he promised Kristy he would, but somehow Kristy's absence preyed on his mind. A good-looking blond, twenty-four-year-old actor should not lack for companionship in a city like New York, but he had little interest in anyone other than Kristy.

She had left a week before "to visit home," she said, and with her bizarrely secretive ways, she wouldn't tell him where "home" was. He'd been unsuccessfully trying, since they'd first met, to find out *something* about Kristy—her heritage, her family, her background— but she simply laughed him off. She called herself his ultimate mystery. She'd smile and ask why, if he loved her—and he did—he needed to know anything more about her? Mark gave up on ever figuring her out. She'd called every day since she left and sounded happy, and Mark tried his best to match her mood.

Even though Kristy had a quarter share in a two-bedroom apartment in Chelsea, they had been living together most of the time since shortly after they met back in November. It had been a hectic half-year, to say the least. First, Lawrence Mickelman had been murdered, and the AWB Company lost its founder and guiding star. Then Ashley Warrington Brunner, eponymous inspiration, financial supporter, occasional actor, and Lawrence's mistress, had been murdered on a tropical island called Illyria, and the company had lost its financial backing. Mark stepped in both times, and through a combination of good luck, perseverance, and the help of a New York City detective by the name of Moriarty, had brought the killers to justice. Through it all, Kristy had been a firm center for him, and being without her, even for this week, threw him off track. With her gone, he couldn't focus, and he'd written but five pages since she'd left. Not good.

Mark's land line rang. He answered it, hoping it was Kristy. "Hello."

No one answered.

"Hello," he repeated. The connection broke off.

Mark put the phone back. The mail should have arrived by now. Besides calling, Kristy had sent him brief emails to reassure him she was thinking about him, but maybe she'd gotten old fashioned and written him a real letter or sent him a humorous "I-Miss-You" card. He grabbed his keys from the dresser top, threw on a pair of jeans, and went the six short flights of stairs to the ground floor. Inside his mailbox, one of the two in the building that still locked, he found two envelopes. One from the friendly telephone company, and rather than a letter from Kristy, he saw a letter addressed *to* Kristy. His detective instincts rose, and he held the envelope up to the light coming through the window of the rusty, never-locked front door of the building. Score one for the post office. The cancellation on the envelope was illegible, and it had slipped through without a return address. He went back upstairs to the apartment.

In all the time Kristy had stayed with him, she'd never gotten mail. No doubt her mail went to the Chelsea apartment. As he tossed the letter on top of his bureau, the phone rang again. This had to be Kristy. He couldn't be thinking about her so constantly without her feeling it.

"Hello," he said.

The person on the other end of the line cleared his throat. "I wonder if I might speak with Kristy King. Is this the correct number?"

"Yes, this is the correct number, but she isn't here right now. Can I give her a message?"

Mark waited while the caller paused. "Can you tell her Richard called? Will she be back soon? I happen to be in the city."

"She won't be back for a while. In fact, she's out of the city. Want to leave a number?"

"Did she go back home?"

The burst of hopefulness in the voice threw Mark off. He managed a weak, "Yes."

"Even better. I'll see her there. Thanks."

"Where is...?"

The phone went dead.

Mark lowered the receiver. Kristy had received phone calls at his apartment before, usually from one of her Chelsea roommates. She'd never gotten a call from a man he didn't know. At least he didn't think she had. Richard?

Mark walked over to the dresser and lifted the letter. He took it to the window and held it up to the light again, looking for a signature. He could see the letter inside the envelope, but it was folded over too often to allow him to spy out the author's name.

Ah, well. Kristy would call soon, and he'd ask her. That possibility whirled around his mind a few times before grinding to a halt. He knew she wouldn't tell him anything. She never told him anything he didn't already know. What had at first been an intriguing aspect of a playful personality now annoyed him.

The phone rang later in the afternoon and, finally, he heard Kristy's voice.

"Were you sleeping?" she asked. "You sound groggy."

"As a matter of fact, I was. How are you?"

"Just fine. You?"

Mark sat up in bed and pulled a pillow behind him. "Half awake. I hoped you'd call earlier."

"I just got back in from taking a walk."

"Down by the riverside?"

Kristy laughed. "Let's see. Does my hometown have a river? Could be? How about a walk down by the old mill stream?"

"Come on. Where are you?"

"Home."

Mark shook his head. Forget it. "When will you be coming...may I say 'home'?"

"You may. I'll be back by the weekend. Two days. Satisfied?"

"The sooner the better."

"I miss you. Don't think I don't."

"And I miss you. You got a letter."

"In what sport? Kissing or hugging?"

"In the mail, comedian."

"One of my roommates bring it over?"

"No. It arrived here addressed to you."

Kristy didn't respond.

"And a fellow named Richard phoned looking for you."

"Oh." The sparkle drained from Kristy's voice.

"Who's Richard? Do I know him?"

"No, no. What did you tell him?"

"I said you were visiting home."

"Well, it doesn't matter. I'll be back on Friday."

"What time?"

"In the afternoon. Will you be in the apartment around five?"

"I will now. I'll look forward to seeing you. Dinner in Phebe's on me."

"Mark, if Richard calls again, tell him you don't know when I'll be back in New York."

"If you want."

"I do. Thanks. See you Friday. Love you. Bye."

"Love you, too. Bye."

Mark stared at the receiver a moment before hanging up. Kristy would have to explain that conversation a bit more fully for him.

He managed a handful of pages at his computer as he tried to work up the murder of Lawrence Mickelman into a novel. He couldn't decide what approach to take. The narrative voice perplexed him. He'd begun it one way and now tried a different approach. He'd try both versions on Kristy when she got back.

Mark was about to head out the door to Phebe's Restaurant, the local actor's hangout, for an inexpensive dinner when the phone rang again. He frowned and went back to pick it up. Kristy again.

"I can't make it back home when I said I would."

"Not this Friday?"

"No."

"Richard got in touch with you then."

"What does that mean?"

A pang of emotion slashed through Mark. Anger? Jealousy? "Did he?"

"Whether he did or not..." Defensiveness riddled Kristy's tone. "I just can't make it. Something came up. I'll need a few more days here."

"Here, where?"

"Mark, please."

"Okay, okay. How much longer, you think?"

"A few days is all. What were you doing?"

"On my way out to Phebe's. I haven't been out a lot this past week, so I figured I'd splurge."

"Wednesday's not a busy night there."

"I'm not looking for company, only a change of scene and some food I didn't cook." An awkward pause followed. "Want me to mail your letter to you?"

"You're cute. Very cute. I'll be back after the weekend to get it."

"I can steam it open and read it to you."

"Now you're not so cute."

"Only kidding, of course. All right. Get done what you have to get done."

"I will. See you then."

He looked over his none-too-attractive apartment. They'd hung up this time without an exchange of love vows. Suddenly, the prospect of Phebe's grew stale. He didn't want to see anybody he knew. Maybe a walk would do...a walk and some Scotch. Single malt Scotch. The Mets-Phillies game on TV. He'd grown fond of Dalwhinie, a single malt Mr. Gehring, the lawyer for the acting company, had introduced him to back in January in the midst of the troubles surrounding Ashley's murder, but he'd finished the two bottles Gehring had given him from Ashley's supply. He went to his dresser and looked in the ceramic box with the Mayan design on the lid where he kept his ready cash. Seventy dollars. He had thirty plus in his pocket. He'd spent next to nothing this past week without Kristy.

Hell, I can afford it. A seventy-dollar bottle of happiness would be the best friend he could find for the next few days. He missed Don. Don Lovett had been a principal actor in the AWB Company and Mark's best friend. Don had accepted an offer from Hollywood and was now involved in a movie of some kind. Even Don, himself, couldn't tell him exactly what it was about, but according to the emails he'd sent Mark, he didn't care. Don was where he wanted to be, doing what he wanted to do.

Where the hell did *he* want to be, and what did *he* want to do? Lie naked next to Kristy topped his list, but since he could not perform the impossible, he settled for the possible. Astor Wines and Spirits and a bottle of Dalwhinie. He stuffed his cash into his pocket and left the apartment.

Two

"It's hard to believe I missed a place that looks like this," said Kristy the following Wednesday, giving Mark's decrepit apartment a dramatic inspection.

"What did you bring me?" Mark asked as he put Kristy's suitcase on the floor next to the bed. She'd arrived by taxi, and Mark didn't know whether from the airport or the bus terminal or from Brooklyn.

"I brought you two of these." Kristy lifted her shirt over her head.

"Uh oh! Sorry, wrong size. I take large."

"You shit."

Mark took her in his arms, and they fell on the bed laughing. Mark lifted his head from Kristy's chest for a moment. "You're in a cheerful mood."

"You're what I love most, Mark." She lay back on the bed and looked into his eyes.

"Hey, that sounded overly serious."

She lifted her head to kiss him and then smiled softly. She lay back down, put her hand behind his head, and pulled it gently toward her. "Shh. We'll talk later. Do your job."

~ * ~

"You must have been saving up," said Kristy, catching her breath.

"You, too." Mark rolled onto his side and draped an arm and a leg across her.

"You know I was almost run down on my visit home."

"Want me to get you some Flintstone's multi-vitamins? Chewable."

"No, no, silly. I mean by a car, a hit-and-run car, no less."

Mark raised his head and rested it on his hand. "Really? How close is almost?"

"Real close. I moved; he didn't."

"He? You saw who was driving the car?"

"It looked like George Bush to me. The younger."

"W?"

"That's who it looked like. I was crossing the street and the car came from nowhere. I barely got out of the way. If I hadn't jumped back..."

"You think he didn't see you?"

"I don't see how he could have missed me. Missed seeing me, that is, but thank goodness he *did* miss me with the car. No thanks to him; he kept right on going. And I swear it looked like George Bush behind the wheel."

"Were you in Texas? Did you get the license number?"

Kristy chuckled. "I was *not* in Texas, and it happened too fast. I couldn't even tell you whether it even *had* a license plate. I saw the car and jumped back, and the car kept going. That was the whole event."

"You must come from a bloodthirsty town."

"Or city. Or village. Or, or, or." She laughed.

Mark lifted his arm away. "I have to go to the bathroom."

When Mark returned, Kristy stood naked by his bureau reading the letter she'd received.

"Not bad news, I hope," said Mark, crawling back into bed and pulling a sheet over him. He put his hands behind his head and studied Kristy. Her skin was a shade darker than it should be after a long winter. Her tropical island tan had long faded. Her black hair hung well down her back. Mark could never pry any genealogical information out of her, but he loved her, his beautiful question mark.

Kristy hadn't answered him about the letter, so he tried again. "From Richard?"

She folded the letter and replaced it in the envelope, picked up her jeans from the floor, and slid the letter into a back pocket. She tossed the pants across the back of one of the room's wooden dining chairs.

"Yes, from Richard."

"How did he get your address here?"

"Someone in the Chelsea apartment gave it to him, I suppose."

"Did he find you back home?"

Kristy waved her hand dismissively. She slid into bed next to Mark. "An old friend."

"He sounded desperately in love with you on the phone."

Kristy frowned. "What's wrong with you?"

"Me? Nothing."

"He's an old friend who wanted to say hello."

"So he said hello?"

"He did."

"And that's it with Richard?"

"Forget about Richard, will you?"

"Yes, dear." The telephone rang. "You or me?"

"You."

Kristy's foolery had diminished considerably with the mention of Richard. He reached across her for the phone.

"Hello?" He listened a moment before covering the mouthpiece. "It's for you. A fellow named Richard."

Kristy looked at him angrily.

"It is, Kristy. You want me to tell him you're not here?"

Kristy shushed him hotly and sprang from the bed. She took the phone with an abrupt thrust of her arm and walked off a few steps. "Yes, Richard?"

Mark assumed a sitting position and listened to Kristy's half of the conversation.

"No, it's not really a good idea. I told you it wouldn't be. No, not much point at all. When do you have to be here? Well, I'll think about it. I said I'd think about it. Yes, here is fine. Yes, yes, yes. Good-bye." She walked back to the bed and hung up. She pursed her lips a moment and said, "All right, already. He's an old boyfriend who doesn't want to accept it's over."

"But it *is* over."

"Yes, very over. Dead and buried over. Decayed to a skeleton over."

"He's persistent."

Kristy twisted one hand in front of her. "I am trying not to be... uncivilized toward him. We've known each other a long time."

"I'm not asking," said Mark, lifting both hands in innocence.

"No, but you're dying to know," said Kristy.

Kristy smiled, and Mark knew what caused it—his retreat from prodding for information. See how long her smile lasted if he made a point of finding out all he could about this Richard. He considered himself too smart—or to be more exact, too cowardly—to press forward. "I love you exactly the way you are, woman of mystery, incomparable lover, and my best friend."

Kristy's smile grew. "Sometimes you say the sweetest things. I think you should be rewarded."

Mark preferred a playful, sweet lover about whom he knew little to a sour, hostile woman with her hackles up joining him in battle. But a dark patch had formed between them, and he didn't know for how long playful and sweet would do it for him. Kristy slid next to him again.

"When you finish with me, darling," said Mark, "I have a few things I'd like you to read."

"You've been working!"

"A little."

"I'll compensate for your working a little by my working a lot." Kristy kept her promise.

Three

Mark hung up the phone on a lazy Saturday afternoon near the end of June and sat next to Kristy, who lay in bed reading. He and Kristy had been together nearly every moment since the call from Richard some three weeks earlier, and Mark's security index had risen considerably. He reached over and pushed Kristy's book down.

"What?" she asked.

"I was thinking. I don't know why we close the theater down in May. No one goes away. It's not like we head out to the Hamptons or the Jersey shore for the summer."

"When will he be here?" asked Kristy. The call had come from Marty Schonbaum, widower, and retired English professor from Drew University in New Jersey, who had gotten himself a respectable two-bedroom apartment on Third Street and immersed himself in the downtown theater life of Manhattan. His retirement income made possible a fantasy his heart and mind made a necessity. He'd become increasingly involved with AWB during the recent season, especially since the demise of its two founders, and his call had been about planning the next production.

"He's coming over. Fifteen...twenty minutes."

"You told him to bring a pint of Scotch?"

Mark shrugged. "He asked if he could bring anything. Maybe I'll go out for some Chinese food later."

When Marty arrived, he handed Mark a thin brown bag. Mark took out the pint bottle.

"Ah," he said, "good old Dewar's." He knew not to expect Dalwhinie, but he was disappointed anyway. "I hope you drink this, too."

"I do, but usually later in the day," said Marty. "Let's get down to—"

The phone rang. Kristy put her book down and picked up.

Marty went on. "Let's get down to business. I've talked to Tony." Tony Babbitte was one of the four permanent members of the troupe who drew a paycheck. "He's ready to get back into harness. Me, too. How about you folks?"

Mark tried to answer and listen in on Kristy's conversation at the same time. "I said to Kristy earlier I don't see why we even stop playing. No one goes anywhere. Acting is all any of us likes to do. Sure, I'm ready, and we have to start thinking of keeping the theater going financially." Ashley's will had not provided the continuing support they would have liked. With scrimping, they could get at least two plays into a new season and hope those plays generated enough income to see the season through. "Marty, it's only right you get on board with us as a permanent member and draw the stipend. We're budgeted for five actors, and Don's share's available."

"Well, it's kind of you, but as a retired college professor I draw a tidy pension. I'm doing what I like. The theater needs the money more than I do, and, to tell the truth, I prefer my freedom. I may want to do a little traveling soon. See some plays in London."

"Your call, Marty." Mark opened the bottle of Dewar's. "It's later in the day than when you arrived. Nearly five o'clock. Almost six in Nova Scotia."

Marty laughed and held two fingers a short distance apart. "Can't argue that. Just a touch."

Mark had both his windows open, and like good New Yorkers he, Kristy, and Marty acted as if the noise from the street didn't exist. Mark sat at his all-purpose wooden dining table in cut-off shorts and an AWB T-shirt. Marty, his professorial days ingrained in him, wore light tan slacks and a short-sleeved shirt, open at the neck. Mark poured two short Scotches.

"So what do you think?" said Mark, sipping from his glass. He'd added ice to Marty's drink, but not to his own.

Marty lifted his drink toward Mark before sipping. "Our new season," he toasted. "I think we should do as you suggested when we parted back in May. Start off with some Shakespeare. We've done a tragedy, *Hamlet*, and a comedy, *Twelfth Night*, why don't we try a history?"

"Stay with Shakespeare, eh?"

"Why not? We like doing Will, and we're good at it."

Kristy hung up and approached the table. "Mark, I have to go out tonight." She gestured her helplessness. "You know who. I'll get it over with as fast as I can."

Mark nodded, although a small bolt of emotion joggled his stomach. Despite his desire to know, the more Kristy's outside life became part of *his* life, the more it discomforted him. He was glad he'd told Marty to bring the bottle of Scotch. "Okay, take your time. Marty and I'll work on things here a while. Maybe we'll end up at Phebe's?"

"I have nothing on tonight," said Marty.

"Good." Mark looked at Kristy. "Maybe you can make it there later."

"If I can, I will. I'll shower and change in the bathroom, Marty. Stay put."

"Not much room here," Marty said, smiling. "I can go out for a walk."

Kristy gathered up what she needed and reassured Marty. "No, no. It's no problem."

"Marty, I know the play we should do," said Mark.

"Yes?"

"How does *Richard Third* sound to you?"

"I love it. Will you play Richard?"

Kristy slammed the bureau drawer a little harder than necessary.

"No, I'm not a Richard kind of guy. I think Tony would love to do a lead role. He hasn't had one yet."

"He *would* love it. I know he would. How about I give him a call and ask him to meet us at Phebe's."

"Sure, and then we can work on the Dewar's and talk about it a while." Marty got out his cell phone and made the call.

Kristy, walking toward the hallway leading to the bathroom, looked back over her shoulder. Mark smiled at her, but she did not return the smile.

~ * ~

Mark got back to his empty apartment from Phebe's at one a.m. He'd stayed late, hoping Kristy would finally get free of Richard and show up, but she hadn't. Now, he lay in bed wondering whether he should call her...be angry with her, be trusting of her, hate Richard, or bask in his role of secure lover. The swirl of possibilities kept him sleepless. By two-thirty, he'd given up on hearing the key in the door and proceeded to pass the night fitfully.

He remained in bed until ten o'clock next morning. Kristy knew he'd be in the apartment and knew he'd be...if not worrying, then wondering. Finally, after he'd made his trip to the deli for coffee and a bagel and gotten halfway through the Sunday *Times*, the phone rang. He moved quickly to the phone, but let it ring once more. "Hello."

"It's me, Mark."

"Well, how are you? *Where* are you?"

"At my apartment."

"Alone?"

"Mark. Don't be unusual. I had my talk with Richard. I made myself clear. I'm sorry it took so long. I didn't want it to. It was so late I decided to come back here."

"How long are you staying in Chelsea? Marty and I decided to get us back to work."

"I heard. *Richard Third.*"

"It's a great play."

"Not for a woman."

"Sure it is. You play the right role, you get to spit on a prince."

"*You're* not playing Richard. I heard you say so."

Mark gave a quick laugh. "Ouch. Let's not get testy, but, yes, Marty and I decided we'd go with *Richard* for the first six or eight weeks and then fold in something more for you and Karen when the season gets officially under way. Talk to Karen. See what you'd both like to do." Karen Christenson was the fourth permanent member of the troupe.

"That sounds better." Mark waited for Kristy to say more, maybe even give him a report on the previous night, but all he got was, "I have a few things to do here. Let's meet at Phebe's tomorrow night. I'll call Karen and tell her to come in. Maybe the whole troupe can get together."

"Good idea. But does it have to be as long as tomorrow night? Can't you finish whatever it is today?"

"Mark, it's the chores I usually have to do. Laundry, the bank. Stuff, you know. I'll see you tomorrow. And don't be sitting there imagining things."

"Last thing on my mind."

"Right. Bye."

Mark went back to the Sunday *Times*, but an hour later he got another call from Kristy.

"Mark, I need your help."

"Calm down. Calm down. What the hell happened in the last hour?"

"My mom called. I'm glad she found me."

So she's got a mother. Mark kept quiet as information came thick and fast.

"My brother Brian's been hurt. He's in the hospital. It happened earlier this morning."

"Oh, I'm sorry. What do you want me to do?"

"I'm going back home again. Can you come with me?"

"Oh! Sure. Where are we going?"

"A small town in Pennsylvania. You wouldn't know it. Brunton?"

"Brunton, Pennsylvania?"

"Yes."

"New to me. Will you come back here?"

"No, I'm packing some stuff now. Can you meet me at my apartment?"

"Sure. How are we traveling?"

"I'll rent a car."

Mark's eyebrows lifted. Not many penurious actors would so blithely do that. He would probably learn a lot about Kristy over the next few days. "I'll pack some things myself and take a cab over. How did your brother get hurt?"

"He was hit by a car."

"Hit by a car? What the hell kind of drivers do you have in this Brunton?"

"I don't know. Hurry over. Thanks. Bye."

Mark hung up the phone, excitement and fear beginning a furious tango in his stomach. It might have been better to remain in blissful ignorance about Kristy's other life, but his ignorance, blissful or not, would soon end. As he threw some things into a suitcase, he replayed Kristy's voice in his mind.

"He was hit by a car."

It made him uneasy. After making certain he had enough money for a taxi, he hurried down to the street.

Four

Claiming she was too upset to drive, Kristy handed the keys for the dark blue Chevy Impala to Mark. He felt uncertain whether it was an appropriate time to pry, yet he couldn't help but ask, "So what exactly happened?"

"Mom said Brian left the warehouse and was on his way back home."

"He works in a warehouse? On a Sunday morning?"

"We *own* the warehouse. He was visiting my mom, and he told her he had to go and check on something. The warehouse is walking distance from the house. It's a small town."

"Was he alone?"

"Yes. Nobody witnessed the accident—at least nobody's said so yet—but a police car found Brian on the ground and called an ambulance. Mom said he's hurt badly."

Mark eased the Chevy into traffic. "What's in the warehouse?"

"Something near and dear to your heart."

"Kristy dolls?"

"No. Liquor."

"Ah! Are you and your brother close?"

"I'd say so. He's older than I am. Twenty-nine."

"You're twenty-nine?"

"Him, Mark, darling. Him."

"Just trying to get you to smile."

Kristy reached a hand across and squeezed his leg.

"Radio okay?" he asked.

"Sure."

Mark found some music and drove on.

~ * ~

"Very pretty place," said Mark as he drove down the main street of Brunton, appropriately named Main Street. Brunton turned out to be a town of some seven thousand people nestled in a very green section of southeastern Pennsylvania.

"I lived here my whole life until New York beckoned. Drive slowly. The cops here get bored easily and look for things to do."

Mark eased up on the gas. "Why did New York beckon?"

"My dad died, oddly enough in a car accident. I'd stayed around when he was alive and done some work in the business as well as some acting, too, but only in the immediate area—in Philadelphia a couple times. My house is a little way outside of town." Kristy pointed. "There's the office, in the back of the store. The warehouse is the building behind it."

Mark looked at a corner, three-story building with a liquor store on the ground floor. Over the liquor store door hung a sign. *King Liquors.*

"Your father owned a liquor store? That satisfies half the requirement of the ideal woman."

Kristy ignored the comment. "The company does wholesale, retail, importing. That's our only store, but we supply I don't know how many others. My brother would have known."

Mark glanced over and saw Kristy's eyes filling. "We're at the edge of town," he said. "Not far now, I presume."

"Yes, almost there."

A moment later, Kristy directed him into the driveway of a large, older home, complete with white siding and happy looking yellow shutters. Three cars lined the long driveway, and others filled the street in front of the house.

"Oh, Mark, I'm frightened. Why are so many cars here?"

"Don't be upset," said Mark, leaving the car and walking around to help Kristy. She got out on her own, though, and Mark followed her along the pebbled pathway to the side of the house. A woman in her early fifties with long black hair streaked with gray opened the door. She dressed stylishly in a deep blue skirt, white blouse, and dark blue high-heeled shoes.

"Oh, Mom," cried Kristy.

Mark followed Kristy into a large kitchen and stood aside as mother and daughter embraced. Kristy's mom had an even more pronounced mix of blood than her daughter. Certainly Asian. Mrs. King took her daughter by the shoulders and moved her back.

"We've lost him, Kristy, darling. We've lost him. He's gone."

Kristy burst into sobs, and her mother embraced her again. Mark retreated further and leaned against the kitchen counter, but right away he felt his posture disrespectful. He stood up straight, hands clasped in front of him, and waited.

There were numerous people in the house, some of whom spilled over into the kitchen to witness the sad family reunion. "When did it happen, Mom?" asked Kristy, rubbing the back of her right hand across her right eye.

"Only an hour ago, darling. Dr. Stone called. I had come home to wait for you, so we could go back to the hospital together, but now..." The two women embraced tearfully again.

Mark noticed one young man with slicked back hair, immaculately dressed in a dark suit, white shirt, and blue striped tie, studying him. For a brief moment, their eyes met and held. Mark sensed a challenge in the gaze and held the gaze much longer than polite. Richard. It had to be Richard. The man strode toward the still-embracing women. He tapped Kristy's mother on the shoulder and, as if cutting in at a high school dance, claimed Kristy from her. They embraced.

"Kristy, sweetheart, if there's anything I can do. Your mom has already asked me to make the proper arrangements, and I'll need your help."

Kristy nodded as she stepped back. Her eyes went to Mark. Richard noticed her glance and said, "Why don't we go back into the living room?" People responded and the buzz of conversation recommenced. Kristy touched Richard on the elbow and made her way back to Mark. Richard joined the exodus into the living room.

Mark leaned close to Kristy. "I heard, and I'm so sorry."

"I didn't know it would be..."

Mark stopped her. "Shhh. All I need to know is my being here helps you in some way."

Kristy kissed his cheek. "It does. Take me in."

"Do you want to go somewhere else for a while instead? Be alone for a few moments?"

"No, no. I'll stay near Mom."

They were alone in the empty kitchen. "I presume Richard was the fellow who chased everybody in."

"Correct. He's involved with the family business. I'm going to have to tell you more about me than you ever wanted to know, but not now." Kristy's eyes filled again. The small talk had kept grief at bay for only a few moments.

Mark pulled her to him. "It must be terrible," he whispered. "I'll do anything you want." Kristy sobbed, and he tightened his embrace.

Over her shoulder, Richard appeared in the kitchen entrance and glanced their way. When Mark caught his eye, he turned away. Mark kept Kristy in a tight embrace. This guy would be hard to take. Kristy's breathing slowed, so Mark took a step back.

"Join your family, Kristy," he said. "Be strong. Your mom needs to see you strong."

"I'll try." Hand in hand, they went into the living room.

As Kristy went to sit next to her mother, Mark found a small bar in the corner of the room. No one paid any attention to him, so he looked behind the bar. A bottle of Chivas Regal caught his eye. Many of the people in the room had drinks, so Mark poured himself a healthy Scotch.

As he replaced the bottle, Richard approached. "You must be Mark Louis," he said.

"I am."

"My name is Richard Sutor, which I once was to Kristy. I spell it without an 'I.' I worked for her father and, until today, her brother."

His tasteless jibe repelled Mark, but he merely responded, "In the liquor business?"

"Yes. Kristy didn't tell you?'

He'd slipped. He didn't want this man to know what Kristy had told him and what she hadn't. "She did. I never realized the size of the business."

"Pretty prosperous. Pretty prosperous."

"What happened today?" Mark sipped from his drink and checked on Kristy, who sat on the sofa with an arm across her mother's shoulders.

"I only know what Betty told me. Brian left the warehouse to come back here, and a car hit him and kept going. No one saw what happened. The police took him right to the hospital."

"Was he conscious?"

"I don't know?'

"Did Brian have a chance to speak to anyone at any time?"

Richard shrugged. "I really don't know. Certainly not to anyone here. I drove back from New York early this morning. Betty called me at home, and I came right over. She wanted to wait for Kristy and then go to the hospital. She expected to see Brian after surgery. Far as I know, Brian never regained consciousness."

"I see. Kristy rented a car, and we started out as soon as her mother called."

Kristy and her mother joined the two men. "Mark, I'd like you to meet my mother. Mom, this is Mark Louis. We work together in the acting company."

"Mark, Kristy has spoken of you. Thank you for coming along with her. It's very kind of you." They shook hands.

"I'm sorry we have to meet under these circumstances, Mrs. King."

"Betty. Please call me Betty."

Someone tapped Richard on the shoulder. "The undertaker is here."

The small talk withered, and grief marched over everyone.

"Kristy," said Richard. "Betty, I'll be back for you when everything's arranged. You'll want to know what we've done." Kristy and Richard walked off.

"How long have you known my daughter?" Mark moved aside as Betty sat on one of the two stools in front of the bar. "There must be some Scotch somewhere," she said. "Can you, please?"

Mark indicated his glass. "There is. Underneath. I'll get it for you." He went behind the bar and lifted the Chivas to the bar top. "This okay?"

"Yes."

"Ice? Neat?"

"Is it what you're drinking?"

"Yes."

"Neat, if you please."

Mark fixed the drink and passed it to the handsome woman.

"How long have you known my daughter?"

Betty's ability to chitchat at a time like this surprised him. He supposed it helped get her through it all, and if she could do it, so could he.

"Kristy joined the company back around November."

"And you and she have been an item...how long?"

"I'd seen Kristy in the neighborhood since the beginning of the year—the theater year. September. I finally met her in November, and we've been good friends since."

Betty took a deep swallow from her glass. "I was not in favor of my daughter going off to New York City, but when her father died, she lost interest in life in Brunton. She left everything, her place in the company, her family—"

Mark finished the sentence for her. "And Richard?"

Betty averted her eyes. "And Richard."

"Kristy says she's known him for quite a long time."

"Since high school. He was a good friend of...Brian's."

Mark glanced away momentarily as the woman struggled to stay composed. She took a second strong sip, drinking her Scotch as if accustomed to it. She made no taking-her-medicine-at-a-bad-time face when it went down. Her eyes closed as she took a third sip, allowing Mark to study her more closely. Kristy's beautiful shape clearly had come from good genes.

Betty opened her eyes, took a deep breath and asked, "Is she doing well in New York? Does she seem happy? I know of no one else to ask."

Mark pulled the second stool further back and sat on it. "She's worked steadily this past year. We invited her into our company, the AWB Theatre Company. It gives her a modest income."

A puff of air burst from Betty's lips. "Income is the least of Kristy's problems. Go on."

"And...I'm happy being with her. I think it's mutual. She enjoys the world she's entered."

"I'm glad to hear it. She tells me the same thing, but..." She lifted two fingers from her glass in a gesture of doubt.

Kristy walked up to them. "Mom, come now."

Betty reached a hand toward Mark and squeezed his wrist.

"Kristy," said Mark. "I think I'll go for a little walk while you take care of what you have to."

"Don't get lost."

"I won't." He took his final sip of Scotch as Kristy and her mother walked away. He put the glass down on top of the bar and noticed three photos hanging on the wall. One clearly showed Kristy, her brother, and parents. She looked in her late teenage years. The other two photos were of couples much older. A white man and Asian woman composed one couple...a white man and woman the other.

The grandparents. So Kristy's mother is half Asian. That made Kristy one-fourth Asian and explained her features. He'd plugged a large piece of puzzle into a wide void. He checked his watch. Four-ten. He planned to walk back to the scene of the accident. Both brother and sister encountering hit-and-run drivers, and one struck and killed. He knew what to look for and only hoped he found it.

Five

...And therefore, since I cannot prove a lover,
To entertain these fair well-spoken days,
I am determined to prove a villain,
And hate the idle pleasures of these days.
Plots have I laid, inductions dangerous,
By drunken prophecies, libels, and dreams...

Tony Babbitte stopped mid-soliloquy. "How do I sound?"

"You sound great, Tony," Mark reported from his seat in the third row of the Bouwerie Lane Theatre as he listened to Tony go through some of Richard's major speeches. "You don't have anything to worry about. You're more than ready for this role."

"Damn," said Tony, jumping down the two feet from the stage. "I don't feel right. I don't feel like Richard. Really, I don't get him yet."

Mark laughed. "It's only the first day we've tried anything with the play, Tony. We haven't even hired any other actors. There's no pressure on you. Relax. What you've read has been fine. I can give you Olivier's movie version. Don borrowed a couple of my *Hamlet*

DVDs when he did *Hamlet*. He said it helped him, especially the Nicol Williamson version."

"Yeah, good idea. Anything to get more ideas."

"We won't be opening until sometime in August, so relax."

"Right, right. I have plenty of time. I'll get it. I know I'll get it." Tony leapt back onto the stage and began again.

Kristy popped from behind the curtains and tiptoed downstage left, keeping an eye on the orating Tony. She lowered herself to the floor and took a seat next to Mark.

"How's he doing?" she whispered.

"He's doing great. I can't remember ever seeing him so excited."

"Excited? Tony? Mr. Cool?"

"He's like a hummingbird. What time is it?"

Kristy waggled her wrist in the dim light until she could see the dial. "Five forty-five."

"Enough of this for today. Let's go across the street. I want to talk to you."

It was Thursday, the day after Brian King's funeral. Mark had stayed in Brunton with Kristy until that morning, when they drove back to New York. They'd had a quick lunch and gone right to the theater. Mark had summoned the permanent troupe and thrashed out the choice of roles each wanted in *Richard III*. In addition, he'd spent a lot of time assuring Tony the role of the murderous king suited him perfectly.

In Phebe's, three men sat separately at the bar, and eight other people were scattered at three tables. Mark and Kristy chose a small table near the dormant fireplace.

"How are you feeling?" asked Mark. "Reasonably back into the world?"

"It's hard to believe...what's happened. It happened so fast. A month ago, I visited with Brian, and now he's gone. It's...unbelievable. I'm okay. I think I'm okay."

Mark handed Kristy a menu. "Your mother is really something. She cried those couple times at the house the first day and then, for one moment, at the cemetery. She's tough."

"You didn't hear her each night when she went to bed. I did. I went in to her. She's very composed in public. Always has been. Undaunted, unflappable, in control. It's the way she is. I'm surprised she let Richard handle so many details of the funeral. I think she did it for my benefit."

"Your benefit?"

Kristy put the menu back on the table without looking at it. "So I could see Richard...taking care of the family."

"Your mother wants him to take care of you."

"True."

"He wants to take care of you."

"Very true."

"But you're too much in love with me."

"Truest of all."

"I have a reason I wanted you alone for a time. It may only be the way my mind works, but there is something I have to tell you."

"So tell me."

A waiter finally appeared, and after Kristy rejected dinner for the moment, Mark ordered a bottle of white wine and some appetizers.

"White," Kristy commented. "You're unusually attentive to my drinking habits. You usually get red. I might want to keep Richard around more in the future."

"You do and I'll use the empty wine bottles to lump up his head."

"Jealousy is such an attractive quality in you."

Mark waved his hand. He needed the playful chatter to stop. "Listen to me."

"Go on."

"When you and Richard and your mother went off to plan the funeral the day we arrived, I went for a walk."

"I remember."

"I went back to poke around outside the store and the warehouse."

"I didn't know you *went* anywhere. I thought you wanted to stay out of the way for a while."

"Tell me what happened when the car almost hit you. It probably happened near the warehouse, too, I'll bet."

Kristy cocked her head. "I'd just left the office. How did you know?"

"It's very quiet back there—off the main hub."

"So?"

"Tell me what happened."

Tiny lines formed above Kristy's nose. "I started across the street and, I don't know, the car appeared."

"Didn't you see it coming?"

"No, it simply loomed up quickly. It shocked me."

"And what did you do?"

"I got back onto the sidewalk real quick."

"Did the car slow down?"

"It kept going. The driver didn't stop."

"I mean did it slow down when you were in front of it? Did the driver hit the brakes? Do you remember the tires squealing?"

Kristy closed her eyes briefly. "No, I don't remember any sound, except maybe the whiz of the car going by. I remember the side view mirror almost clipping me. What's your point? You're making me tense."

Mark squirmed a bit on his chair as he reached the key point of his conversation. "I went back to the warehouse. I could figure out the route your brother would have taken, and I looked everywhere for tire marks. Skid marks."

"And?"

"I didn't find any."

"So?"

"So the driver didn't hit his brakes. He or she didn't notice your brother, slam on the brakes, and try to swerve aside. It doesn't seem as if your driver tried to avoid you either."

Kristy's voice took on an edge. "What are you saying?"

Mark looked down, unwilling to meet Kristy's eyes. When he looked at her again, he lifted a dubious hand. "I think it's a strange set of circumstances where the same thing happened to each of you."

Kristy sat close-mouthed.

Mark went on. "The odds would be very high against it happening twice, don't you think?"

Finally, Kristy answered with great deliberation. "No. No, I don't think. Mine...just a quick thing. Me not paying attention. Brian's was an accident. The driver got frightened, panicked, and kept going."

"Maybe," said Mark as the waiter arrived with the wine. He filled Kristy's glass and then his own. "Drink up."

Kristy ignored the wine. "Why do you bring up something like this when you know it would upset me?"

"Are you upset?"

"Yes, I'm upset. Now!"

Mark looked into his wineglass for a moment. "I need to tell you something else."

"There's more!"

"A little. Nothing much."

Kristy took a breath and glared.

"I wanted to get the police report of your brother's death when we were there, but it would doubtless have been kind of tacky and inappropriate."

"Doubtless. It would have been."

"I wish you wouldn't get angry with me."

"I'm not. I'm not." Kristy drank some of her wine.

"It's possible your brother may have said something to the police or in the ambulance before he lost consciousness."

"Why are you doing this?"

Mark's stomach danced a tango as Kristy's sad eyes bore into him. "You sound exasperated with me. It's on my mind because if it wasn't an accident, if both weren't accidents, you may be in danger. You never did get around to telling me any family secrets or the details of your connection with the family and the business and Richard. Would I be correct in saying there's some substantial money involved in your family liquor business?"

"You would be correct."

"Who benefits from your brother's death?"

"Benefits!"

"Financially. Please stay calm. I promise I'll change the topic in a moment."

"What good is changing the topic? You know I'll be thinking about this all night now." Kristy downed the rest of her wine. "My mother and me, who else? My dad owned the whole business. He left it to the three of us, and he groomed my brother to take over. When Dad died, Brian stepped right up."

"Who will run things now?"

"Mom, I suppose. She's always been involved, and she's quite capable of running the company on her own."

"She'll do that? Run the company on her own, the day-to-day nitty-gritty?"

Kristy held her empty wineglass by the stem and spun it slowly. "Probably not. No, Richard will...Mark!" Kristy stopped abruptly, set her lips, and looked hard at Mark. "Is this about Richard?"

"No, no. Don't even think it, but he *will* be the person to take over the day-to-day operation of the business, right?"

"Probably, yes," said Kristy. "But so what?"

"Okay, no more questions. I promise. Here, have a chicken finger."

"I don't want a chicken finger. What are you going to do now?"

"With your chilly tone of voice, I kind of wish they'd get the fireplace going tonight."

"Stop putting me off. What are you going to do now?"

"I'd really like to get the police report."

"And if I say no?"

Mark's eyes widened. "Kristy, it can't hurt. If there's nothing there, I won't bring it up again to you, and we'll feel better knowing there's nothing."

Kristy's voice had steadied. "How will you get the report?"

"I don't think the Brunton police will send it to me, and I don't suppose we're going back to Brunton any time soon. Even if we did, I doubt they'd let me see it, and I wouldn't want to impose on you or your mother to ask such a thing in any case. I can ask Moriarty to try and get it."

Kristy eyes held Mark's. "If you find out anything...anything I should know, you'll tell me?"

"Of course. And I love you."

Kristy sniffed in mild disdain and looked away. "Because you got your way."

"No, because I want to be certain the girl I love isn't in any jeopardy."

Kristy waggled her wineglass. "I'm in jeopardy of being sober. Please?"

Mark gave a little laugh, relieved he'd made it through the conversation. As he poured Kristy's second glass of wine, he asked, "Want to order any dinner?"

"Just some more appetizers'll do. I'll take a chicken finger now."

"Good. Let's enjoy the rest of the evening with no reference to sad tales past." He would call Moriarty first thing next morning.

Six

"You called him already?" Kristy snapped. "Where was I?" She lay in bed in Mark's apartment the next morning watching him dress.

"You were still asleep. I wanted to get this out of the way quickly."

"Now, I'm not so sure I like your idea." Kristy pulled herself up in the bed and stuffed the pillow behind her.

"We had this conversation in Phebe's last night." He'd been trying to dress silently and make his way out without awakening Kristy.

"Why are you in such a hurry?"

"I told you," he said, sitting on his one cushioned living room chair to tie his sneakers. "But you're probably right. The hit and run cars were most likely coincidences." He looked up at her. "But if they weren't, someone may be trying to hurt you. I'd like to read the police report on your brother's death if Moriarty can get it for me. It can't hurt, and I'm a little surprised you're not more interested yourself."

Kristy sat in silence a moment. Mark tied his second sneaker as quickly as he could, but the lace slipped from his jittery fingers, and he had to start over.

"What made you think of doing this?"

Mark straightened up, his sneakers successfully tied. "I told you everything yesterday. The coincidence of it. The lack of tire marks in your brother's case. Your description of the car that missed you not slowing down."

Kristy shook her head slightly and looked down.

Mark walked over to her and knelt beside the bed. "What's bothering you?"

"I don't know. I don't know. Something about your investigating my brother's accident...I don't like it for some reason."

Kristy had on a tank top, size small. It was tight and low over her chest. Mark felt a buzz of arousal stir him.

He got to his feet. "You asked me if this had something to do with Richard. It doesn't. Does your problem with my looking into the police report have something to do with Richard?"

Kristy looked at him, her face going from thoughtful to defensive in a moment.

"That remark wasn't necessary. It simply makes no sense. What time are we due at the theater today?"

"Noon."

"I'll meet you there."

Mark felt the dismissal and was, in part, thankful for it. He left the apartment.

~ * ~

Detective Walter Moriarty was a short, fiftyish, career police officer. He'd become a detective some twenty years before, liked it, and decided to cease his climb up the career ladder. He'd given up exercising and accepted his paunch as appropriate for a New York City detective—a kind of second badge. He and Mark had collaborated twice before when misfortune struck the AWB Theatre Company, and now, shirttail askew, hair falling, as usual, across his forehead, he sat at his desk at the Sixteenth Precinct in downtown Manhattan. He'd gotten Mark's call after he'd arrived at eight that morning and left word for him to be sent right in.

"Mark, nice to see you." The detective stood and came around to the front of his cluttered metal desk. The two men shook hands, and Mark settled onto one of the two wooden chairs in front of the desk. Moriarty went back to his cushioned, green leather swivel chair, pushing in his shirttail as he went.

"I'd like your help with something," said Mark.

"I'm glad you do. Seems you're the only way I ever get to work on something with any pizazz to it. I'm getting weary of this crap." He lifted an untidy pile of papers and returned them to his desk in even greater disarray. "Lots of crime. Lots of crap. Nothing like the stuff you brought me. Hey, weren't we something that night in the basement of your theater?"

Moriarty referred to the one-act drama he and Mark had put on to bring Lawrence Mickelman's murderer out into the open.

Mark grinned. "You don't do stuff like that every day, Detective?"

"Yeah, right." Moriarty tapped the pile of papers again. "Drug murders. Spouse murders. Perp either obvious or impossible to figure out. Nothing devious. No brain power goes into any of this."

"You know, Sherlock Holmes used to complain to Watson about the same thing when things were slow on Baker Street."

"Sherlock Holmes, yeah. Him I heard of. What you got for me today don't involve me reading no more Shakespeare, does it? *Hamlet?* What was the other one? Some night?"

"*Twelfth Night.*"

"Yeah, *Twelfth Night.* You doin' another play now?"

"More Shakespeare," Mark said, smiling. "*Richard Third.* We're going to open in a month or so."

"He a king or something?"

"He committed a string of murders to clear his path to the throne."

Moriarty's eyebrows went up. "I like him already." He glanced at his watch. "I gotta be somewhere in half an hour. What's up?"

Mark explained what had happened and made his request.

"No skid marks, eh? I would've thought of that. I would."

"I'm sure you would, but I'm wondering whether the Brunton police did. I'd like to know what's in their report."

"All right," said Moriarty. "Give me a little bit to think up a story to tell them."

"I already have one for you."

"Go."

"Tell them Brian's sister was the victim of a suspicious hit-and-run incident here in the city, and you want to read their report because you think it's an awfully big coincidence the same thing nearly happening to brother and sister."

"And I know about their event because...?"

"Kristy mentioned it to you when she reported what happened to her."

"Hers happened second then."

"For our purposes."

Moriarty rose. "Brunton, Pennsylvania. Never heard of it. I gotta get going. I'll call you when I talk to them."

"You have my cell number, I know."

"I have your cell, the theater, your apartment, Kristy's place, everyplace. I'm the New York police, remember?"

"Whatever you do, don't call Kristy. This is a touchy subject to her. Call me. I'll be waiting to hear from you."

"Okay, your cell then." The men shook hands and parted.

Mark enjoyed the twenty-minute walk to the theater. He felt, finally, as if he were doing something. He'd set something in motion. Both brother and sister—hit-and-run—money involved. Before too much time went by, he had to sit Kristy down and ask the myriad of questions he had dammed inside him, but he'd let it wait until Moriarty got the report. He'd either have more ammunition to unload on her or no ammunition at all.

As Mark waited to cross Fourteenth Street, a young, cocoa-skinned woman sashayed toward him from across Third Avenue. She wore a yellow halter-top and tight, white shorts. Long brown hair swirled about her shoulders as she scurried to make the light. She passed in front of Mark and, with the new green light, crossed Fourteenth Street ahead of him. He walked behind her, wrapped in the slow enjoyment of her movements. She turned east at Thirteenth Street, and Mark stopped a moment, but sensibly decided to keep going toward the theater. He gave her a final glance before he stepped into the street and continued his way south. New York in the summer.

Probably a million better places to be, but there were compensations. Before he reached the theater, he counted six more women he felt he could be interested in if his attraction to Kristy weren't so strong. Kristy had become so much a part of him, he was merely playing games fantastical, as Shakespeare might have put it, when he inspected other women. Pleasant and harmless.

As he ascended the stairs to the front entrance of the theater, he put the frivolous, make-believe world behind and returned his focus to the more serious make-believe world ahead of him. Auditions began today, and *Richard III* moved forward.

Mark used his key to get in the front door—most of the actors used the basement entrance—because he had a subtle suspicion that as managing director of the theatre, an appearance through the main entrance enhanced his dignity. He walked into the theater itself and stopped short. Kristy sat in the front row right, and next to her, on the aisle, sat a young man with dark, slicked back hair. Even from the rear, Mark recognized him right off. None other than the famous Richard. He strode forward, summoning his full supply of aplomb.

"Hello, Kristy," said Mark, looking at her and nowhere else.

"Oh, hi, Mark. You remember Richard."

Now he gave Richard his attention. "Of course."

Richard stood and extended his hand. Dressed in his seemingly perpetual business attire, his shoes gleamed even in the muted light of the theater.

Mark shook the proffered hand. "Sit," he said, taking a few steps backward himself, and sitting on the edge of the stage. "What brings you to New York?"

"Business. Kristy. We're about to import some Australian wine into the country. Rosemount is the brand. Shiraz is the type of wine. Have you ever had any? It's very good."

"Rosemount Shiraz," Mark tilted his head as if going over an interminable list of wines he had drunk. "No, no. I don't think I have."

"Do you drink wine? I'll bring you some."

"I do," Mark answered, ignoring Kristy's snort. "So does Kristy."

"Terrific. Okay if I leave it here at the theater?"

Mark lifted his hand in acceptance. "By the way," he added, "did you have a chance to get your car fixed up yet?"

Richard's forehead creased. "My car?"

"Didn't you have to get a dent repaired?"

"I did, but how did you know?"

Mark looked at Kristy. "You mentioned it, didn't you, sweetheart?"

Kristy looked daggers at him.

Richard smiled. "Kristy, you told your friend what a klutzy driver I am?"

"I must have mentioned it."

"I still don't know what I was thinking of. Well, maybe I do." He looked at Kristy, whose lips remained tightly closed. "I swung the car around in the lot a little too wide. Bang, into the loading dock, and I'd picked up the car brand new the day before."

Mark nodded sympathetically. "When Kristy visited home, wasn't it?"

"Mark..." Kristy began, but Richard answered.

"Right. What, a couple days before you left?"

"I think so."

"It wasn't much of a dent. I've already had it repaired. No big deal."

The silence lingered until Kristy said, "Marty wants you. I think he wants to go over the audition schedule."

Mark grabbed his chance to leave the threesome gracefully. "Where is he?"

Kristy pointed straight down. The dressing rooms and a patrons' lounge were in the basement of the theater.

Mark said, "I'll go find him."

Richard rose. "I better get going, too. Nice to have seen you again."

Mark stood, then extended his hand and smiled into Richard's eyes until Richard looked down and broke his grasp. Mark turned, hopped up on the stage, and disappeared into the wings. Before reaching the stairway, he paused, and stepped back toward the stage, remaining out of sight. "No," Kristy said. "I won't."

Richard said a few indecipherable things before Mark heard him say, "Tell him."

Kristy said, "No," again, clearly. The two voices sank, and Mark made an undignified dash to the stairway. A moment later, he and Marty Schonbaum sat at a table discussing the rehearsal schedule. Kristy did not join them for another fifteen minutes.

Seven

Mark steered clear of the topic of Richard and discussed only business when Kristy joined him and Marty. Since she wasn't needed to watch the auditions, she left early, and Mark found her waiting for him at the apartment when he got home.

Mark closed the door and started in with a report on the day's progress. "We found a few likely people today." Kristy lay on the bed, fully clothed and shoeless in her jeans and yellow tank top. Her look betokened trouble, but Mark went on. "One odious looking fellow just right for Buckingham."

"You still see yourself as the savior, Henry Tudor?"

"Well, yes. The blond hair and all. It suits me."

"Well, keep salvation for the damned play. You embarrassed the hell out of me today."

"How so?"

Kristy swung her legs over the side of the bed and sat up straight. "What was the bit about Richard getting his car fixed? I didn't tell you we ran into the loading dock at the warehouse."

"I know. I wanted to find out whether he dented his car."

"Why?

Mark shrugged and looked away, intimidated by Kristy's ferocity.

She got to her feet. "You don't think Richard drove those cars, do you? Don't tell me that."

Mark's answered softly, "The thought had crossed my mind."

"Ugh!" Kristy spluttered. "I don't recall the car that almost hit me having a dented fender. It wasn't even the same color. Don't you believe in coincidence? What you imagine isn't possible. I told you I don't want you doing this."

Mark summoned up some backbone. "Well, that's *not* what you told me, and don't you think the dented fender is another coincidence on top of all the others? What kind of an accident did he have? Foolish, I'll bet. 'Oh, I don't know what I was thinking of.' But there's the dent ready to cover up any other dent he might accumulate in the next few days. And remember, he'd changed cars about that time—after you were almost struck."

Kristy walked to the window. "Stop it! Do you know what you're saying? Richard is...a friend of mine."

"Friends can still have secrets from one another. You and I are friends." Mark wanted to bite his tongue.

"What's that supposed to mean?"

"Nothing."

"Don't give me 'nothing.' You said it. What did you mean?"

"Nothing."

"Mark!"

Mark put his finger to his lips. "This is New York, but do keep your voice down."

Kristy stepped nearer. "What secrets? What do you mean?"

"What is it Richard wants you to tell me?"

"What?"

"'What?' So now you're suddenly hearing impaired?" *He* was getting angry. "What are you so worried about? I don't think I'm out of line looking into what happened to your brother. I don't think I'm out of line caring what happens to you. I love you, but you're acting like you're trying to protect Richard. Why don't you sit down and tell me..." Mark waved one hand before him as if trying to brush aside cobwebs in a haunted house. "...a story I can understand? Tell me where everybody stands in dear little Brunton. Who is this Richard, and why are you so all-fired worried about him?"

"He's my husband, Mark."

Mark felt as if someone had slammed him across the back of the head with a tombstone. Every cogent idea in his mind fractured and crumbled into atoms, blown into eternity by Kristy's response. Mark looked at her in speechless pain.

"He's the reason I left Brunton," Kristy said, sitting back down on the bed. "We got married for all the wrong reasons. Family pressure. The family business. To make my mom happy. Stability. Continuity. My dad died two months after the wedding. With him gone, stability, continuity, didn't mean the same thing. My brother took over. Richard worked all day. I hung around the house with my mom a lot. They gave me some things to do at the business, but..." She shook her head. "I left. I told them I was going, and I left. It caused an awful scene, but I had to get out. To tell you the truth, I wanted out before I got pregnant and lost the ability to leave Brunton forever. Richard wanted a baby. My mom wanted to be a grandmother. My brother was still single. Everything fell to me, but I wanted out. I hated it. I even went to the doctor and got a birth control prescription without telling anyone."

"Take a breath," said Mark. He walked numbly to his dining table and pulled out one of the chairs. He sat. "You've been married all this time since I met you?"

Kristy nodded, tight-lipped.

"Do you still...sleep with him? You were home with him."

Kristy looked down.

"You did."

"Once," she said softly. "He doesn't want the divorce to become final, but I swear it will by the end of the summer. He thinks he can change my mind."

"You slept with him when you were home?"

"No, I didn't *sleep* with him. We...I...one afternoon. I don't know why. He was so insistent. I regret it now."

Mark's head began to throb. He couldn't believe this. Thirty minutes ago, he'd happily come from a sweet day at the theater, and now he didn't know what the hell was important to him anymore. He rose from the chair.

"I'm going out," he said.

"You want me to leave?" asked Kristy.

Mark didn't reply. He couldn't face her. He walked toward the apartment door. He didn't know what he wanted other than to be somewhere else.

"Your detective friend called," said Kristy.

Mark refused to respond, pulled the door open, and left.

~ * ~

After he'd walked for nearly an hour, Mark took out his cell and called Moriarty. He knew what he'd hear. The report was cut and dry. Nothing of interest. Forget about Brian's hit and run. There would be nothing to do but jump back into the morass his life had become for wanting the report in the first place.

"Detective Moriarty, please. This is Mark Louis. He's expecting my call."

Mark waited, keeping his mind clear since no thought would bring him any relief.

"Mark?"

"It's me, Detective."

"I got the report faxed to me this afternoon. You busy?"

"Very unbusy."

"Come over. It's got something in it."

"You're kidding. What's it have?"

"You better come and read it."

"On my way."

~ * ~

Moriarty sat at his desk when Mark entered his battered office twenty minutes later. The two shook hands, and Mark took a seat. The detective immediately pushed a manila folder across the desk.

"Let me save you some time," said Moriarty. "It's only got six pages, mostly routine, but go to page five."

Mark found the page and read. Two-thirds of the way down the page, he stopped. "Holy shit."

Moriarty leaned back in his chair. "Holy shit is right. Like you said, coincidences on top of coincidences. Like a freaking layer cake."

Mark read the lines again. "...claimed the car which hit him was driven by someone who looked like the president." The report quoted the rest of the conversation.

Officer Landis: Which president?

Brian King: Bush. George Bush.

Mark closed the folder and let it lie in his lap.

Moriarty rose and walked to the coffee machine in the corner of the room. "Even if we can't prove George Bush was still in Texas on the day in question, I believe we can rule him out as a suspect. Want some coffee?"

Mark answered distractedly. "We can certainly do that. No, no coffee. Can you make a copy of this for me?"

"I can if you keep it quiet."

"I will. If I want to show it to anyone, I'll let you know. Kristy...?"

"She's okay," said Moriarty, "but anybody else, I gotta know beforehand."

Moriarty placed a full coffee cup on his desk and took the file outside to copy it. Mark, left alone for a moment in the office, called home. It rang four times before the machine came on. He waited for his voice to end and asked Kristy to pick up. She didn't, and he hung up. He slumped back in his chair. He had no interest in calling her cell. If she wasn't in the apartment, she didn't want to talk to him. The circumstances of this accident had gone way beyond coincidence. When Moriarty returned, he'd tell him about the dented fender. Richard dented it before he'd ever had to use it. Mark knew he had a long way to go before he could make any sense of this, and whether Kristy liked it or not, he would do the necessary work.

Eight

Auditions continued the following Monday. Mark, Marty, and Tony sat through a number of readings, and Mark felt certain casting would be completed by week's end.

Kristy had not come home since she'd told Mark about Richard. She and Mark occasionally caught each other glancing their respective ways at the theater, but nothing came of it. Mark finally cornered her and asked if they could talk, but Kristy's eyes filled, and she said she needed more time. What the hell did she need the time for? Mark asked himself. To decide whether to go back with him to Avenue B or to be true to Richard? Well, he'd made his overture. The burden was on her shoulders. But why would Kristy be angry with him? What could she possibly be angry at? What the hell had he done?

No rehearsals or auditions were scheduled for the weekend, and Mark spent Saturday at his computer working on his mystery novel about Lawrence's murder. Kristy, though, would not be driven from his mind. Could forgiveness be an issue? Kristy's being married to Richard but wanting to leave him was one thing. It had been a deception on her part, but one he could deal with, especially when a moderate feeling of triumph over Richard arose. Her sexual encounter with Richard did not play so well. *That* he'd have to forgive, if not overtly to Kristy, then inwardly for his own sake. His male ego was in the way, but, hell, what she did *needed* forgiveness. He hadn't slipped and fallen to some other lover. She had. At the moment, whatever he needed to force the two of them to have a conversation—forgiveness, or something else— he lacked. The humiliation of devoting himself to someone who might not deserve it burned inside of him. His dedication to Kristy had been so weakened by events, he half hoped she would *not* approach him. Finding an adequate response to her would be a test.

At six o'clock, he turned the computer off as the first inkling of hunger scratched at him. Seven new pages, a good session. He didn't feel like cooking, but then, when did he ever? He didn't want to go to Phebe's and maybe run into Kristy. Take-out Chinese would serve tonight.

~ * ~

As he crunched down on his fortune cookie an hour later, he decided he'd put things off long enough. First, he opened the nine-dollar bottle of Montpelier Merlot he'd treated himself to—a bottle that cost as much as his usual 1.5 L. bottle of Frontera, twice its size. He turned on the fan in his apartment and aimed it at the bed. He put the wine bottle on the night table next to him and, clad in running shorts, he piled the pillows behind him and sat back. The topic for the rest of the evening would be—what should he do about Brian King's death? He had not eliminated the possibility of foul play. Both drivers looking like George Bush had linked the hit-and-run attempts on Kristy and Brian into an inextricable knot. Had Richard hired someone? Dangerous approach to let someone else in on such a thing. Did Richard drive around in a rubber mask? Mark had seen such masks in stores. Or did it have nothing to do with Richard at all? Had an unknown someone set out to hurt the King family? No, nothing he'd learned so far led him in that direction. He wanted more information about Richard. Kristy wouldn't help him. The only other possibility— Kristy's mom, Betty. Mark refilled his glass. Okay, he'd found a *who* to help him. The next portion of the wine bottle would help decide *how* to make his approach. He sipped. Face-to-face. It would be easier and less stressful to do over the phone, but this *had* to be done face-to-face. It would add a necessary gravitas to the encounter, plus he could better gauge Betty's reactions if he saw her react. He'd have to make a trip to Brunton. He sipped again. So much for *how*. Now, *when*? There was nothing going on in the theater the next day. If Betty consented to speak with him, that would be perfect. He dare not tell her over the phone what he wanted to talk about. He'd say it concerned Kristy and hope Betty's motherly instinct would do the rest. Next, how to get to Brunton, Pennsylvania. Renting a car would fracture his finances for a month at least. Who to borrow a car from? Another sip. Moriarty. Did he work on Sundays? It didn't matter. He wanted Moriarty's car, not Moriarty. Mark closed his eyes as the wine began to hit him. He would finish this glass and make his calls to Moriarty first, then Betty before it got too late. After that, as he finished off the bottle, he'd jot down the questions he wanted to ask Betty King. He might only get one chance at her, and he wanted to be thorough.

~ * ~

Sunday morning at ten o'clock found Mark driving through the outskirts of Brunton. Moriarty did work on Sunday, and Mark met him at the precinct at eight. Mark got his permission to discuss aspects of the Brunton police report, and before Mark got underway, he and Moriarty talked of ways of dealing with Betty King. Moriarty didn't need the car back until six o'clock, so Mark knew he had plenty of time.

Kristy's mom had been cordial on the phone and expressed no qualms about his visit, mysterious as he made it seem. He'd told her Kristy was the topic, and that got him his appointment. The true topic, the death of her son, would need to be broached with some grace and circumspection. Betty King, her long hair collected behind with a thick, white, frilly tie, wore a short tan skirt, a loose white sleeveless blouse, stockings, and white high heels. Mark wished he'd worn something other than jeans and an AWB T-shirt.

"Please, come in, Mark," said Betty. "Have you had breakfast?"

"Some coffee on the way." Mark followed her through the living room and into the bright, sunlit kitchen.

"I thought it might be the way you'd travel," she said, smiling and indicating the kitchen table and an assortment of breakfast cakes on a crystal serving platter. The smell of coffee filled the air. "Please, sit."

Betty crossed the kitchen to the coffeepot. She filled two blue, gold-rimmed mugs and returned to set them on the table. She went to the refrigerator and took out a small, silver pitcher of cream. She was certainly fun to watch. She moved like her daughter.

Sugar, cream, napkins, knives, and forks in place, Betty finally sat. The time for his graceful approach arrived when Betty said, "And for what reason, Mark, did you make this long trip to Brunton? And without Kristy."

"Well, actually I wanted to talk to you *about* Kristy." Mark detected sadness in the face Betty put on for him. "I'm not here asking for her hand in marriage or anything," he said with a small grin. Sure enough, Betty's face relaxed.

"Was I so obvious?" she asked, matching Mark's grin.

Mark lifted his hand dismissively from the table. "It's not important. I should tell you why I need to ask certain questions."

"Maybe we'd be more comfortable in the living room. Bring your cake and coffee with you. Take more, please."

Mark took another Danish and followed Betty, mug and plate in hand, to the living room. He sat in a soft chair that matched the same blue material as the sofa, where Betty sat. She put her coffee mug on the coffee table and indicated Mark should do the same. She crossed her legs and sat back. An appreciable expanse of attractive leg extended from the tan skirt, and Mark focused on her face.

"And how is my daughter?"

"She's moved back to her Chelsea apartment for now."

"Oh?"

"A disagreement. Plus, she told me some things she hadn't told me before, and it will take us both some time to deal with the changed landscape." 'Some *time*.' An echo of Kristy.

"She told you...?"

"About Richard. Her husband."

"Ah. We were under strict orders not to mention the marriage. This has understandably upset you."

Mark shifted his weight. He did not want to discuss how he felt about Richard and Kristy's marriage, so he took the conversation in another direction. "Did Kristy tell you she was almost struck by a car when she stayed with you this summer?"

"No."

Mark noticed a small, vertical line appear between Betty's eyes. "She told me."

"Go on," said Betty.

"She mentioned it to me when she got back from trip. She said the driver looked like President Bush the second."

Puzzlement flashed into Betty's face.

Mark held up his hand. He did not need a reaction from her yet. "Listen. Your son's accident happened a short time later—again a hit-and-run driver. Coincidence? No, listen. When I came to Brunton with Kristy, I walked to the spot of your son's accident. I couldn't find any tire marks, skid marks, which should have been there if the driver had tried to stop the car suddenly. I asked Kristy whether the driver who nearly hit her had slowed down or slammed on the brakes. She said he hadn't." Mark gave Betty time to process.

"Go on," she said.

"Well, I have a friend in New York, a police officer, Detective Moriarty. I asked him if he would get the Brunton police report concerning your son's accident for me. He did."

Betty stiffened. "And?"

"Your son remained conscious briefly and also told the police the man who struck him looked like President Bush."

After a pregnant pause, Betty said, "Are you suggesting... someone tried to hit Kristy and failed, and the same person then went after my son?"

Mark responded quickly. "I'm suggesting there are some unsettling coincidences at work here. I think something may be... going on."

Betty stood and walked across the room. After facing the wall a moment, she turned and faced Mark. "Do you have anything more to tell me?"

"I do."

Betty took a breath and returned reluctantly to the sofa. She glared at Mark and waited.

Mark continued. "I understand from Kristy your liquor business is quite valuable."

"It is."

"With your husband and son gone, you and Kristy are the heirs."

"Of course."

"Is there anyone else who stands to get a substantial share of the business, a promotion, if a couple of occurrences fall his way?"

"*His* way? Richard? You don't mean Richard, do you?"

"Does anyone else stand to benefit?"

Betty settled back, as if relieved the point he had traveled so far to make had proven so flimsy. "I have known, my family has known, Richard all of his life. I knew his father and his grandfather, Richards both," she said with a smile. "As boys, he and Brian played together, went to school together. He and Kristy discovered each other when she was in high school. The company has depended on him for so much for so very long."

"I'd like to ask a few questions about Richard and the company."

"Go right ahead," said Betty.

"What is Richard's position now in the company?"

"Although we haven't discussed it yet, we both know he will become the...we really don't have a title. We print 'President' on the business cards. Looks stylish."

"More salary?"

"Yes."

"A lot more?"

"Yes."

"Any ownership in the company?"

"No." Betty leaned forward and casually swept some crumbs into her hand and then onto her plate.

"The marriage to Kristy. How would it have changed his status?"

"We were preparing to make an adjustment in the organization of the company after they'd married, but they weren't together long enough for the lawyers to complete it."

"And the adjustment?"

"Twenty-five percent ownership."

"How much business does the company do?"

"We can gross nine or ten million dollars in a good year. It varies."

"And Richard's salary?"

"My, we *are* being inquisitive here."

"And confidential."

"Something along the lines of a hundred and fifty thousand, and before you ask, it will go to two hundred soon."

Mark sipped his coffee, but it had grown cold. "What will happen to Richard when the divorce is finalized?"

"He'll continue to work for the company. No change. I think a lot of him."

"Any ownership?"

Betty didn't answer.

"Please tell me," said Mark.

"We've discussed it," said Betty.

"Discussed it?"

Betty took an impatient breath. "I mentioned to him that with his added responsibilities, the time he's spent working for us, how much, personally, he meant to me..."

"You would give him some ownership?"

"He could *buy* some ownership. Lower his salary and take some compensation in the form of ownership."

"What's Kristy's share of the business?"

"My husband left me fifty percent. Kristy and Brian each received twenty-five percent, and now Brian's twenty-five percent will be split."

"Sixty-two and a half for you and thirty-seven and a half for Kristy after the math's done?"

"Yes. Have more cake."

Mark ignored her offer. "You're willing to let Richard have some of your share."

"Ten percent at most. Not enough for me to lose control."

Mark put his coffee cup down.

"That must be cold by now. May I get you more?"

"No, thanks."

"Then may we go back to your original point?" asked Betty.

"That being...?"

"The accident."

"Accidents, plural. Remember, the drivers seem to have been identical."

"And looked like President Bush?" Betty asked, not bothering to conceal her skepticism.

Mark spread his hands. "Someone could have been hired. Or perhaps a mask."

"And to you, Richard seems a logical suspect to be involved?"

Mark explained about the dent Richard put in his car.

"Still another of your coincidences?" Betty asked softly.

"It happened. I hope you can see what I see. Too *many* coincidences."

Betty looked down and shook her head. She refocused her attention on Mark. "I don't really know what to say to you. The concept of Richard Sutor wishing anything but the best for Kristy or for my family is repugnant. Neither my heart nor my head will even consider it." Betty leaned forward and held his gaze. "We surely must promise each other everything we discussed today will remain in this room."

"I readily agree to *that*, Mrs. King."

"Betty, Betty," she said absently. "Have you told this to Kristy?"

"Some, not all. She begrudgingly told me to pursue it, but I didn't know about her connection to Richard then. She's as reluctant as you are to see Richard in another light."

After a moment, Betty said, "I'm thinking...you know, we do have one store like that in town."

"Like what?"

"It's a party goods store. Balloons, special things for birthday gatherings. In October each year, they open a Halloween section. Decorations, costumes. They sell lots of different masks. I remember seeing the display."

"This is the middle of July, almost a year since they would have sold Halloween masks. Where is this store?"

"Elm Street. I'll have to get the address for you."

Betty rose and when she returned, she handed Mark an index card.

Mark glanced at it. "I'll take a look before I leave Brunton."

"May I ask *you* a question?"

"Go ahead."

"I don't quite comprehend why you are so hard at work on my family's problems." Her tone of voice changed. "Does Kristy mean so much to you?"

Mark shifted in his seat. "She does mean a lot to me. I've missed her these past few days, but to be honest, I have to tell you what I told Kristy when she asked practically the same question. It's the way my mind works. If these coincidences are not simply coincidences, Kristy may be in danger." Mark shrugged. "It sounds melodramatic, no doubt, but she *was* almost struck by a car."

A lengthy silence ensued.

Finally, Betty took a deep breath and smiled. "Have you run out of questions?"

Mark smiled back and stood. "For now, but if you think of anything you might have told me and didn't, anything that comes to mind later, I'd like to leave my phone number."

"Kristy gave it to me. I have it."

"My cell?"

"No, give me that. I understand."

Mark provided his cell number. "Well then, I thank you for your time."

Betty walked him to the front door and opened it. She touched his arm as he stepped out. "You will keep in touch with me?"

"If there's anything worth telling you, I'll tell you."

"Thank you. Please, watch out for Kristy. You're the only New York friend of hers I've met."

"I will."

Betty took her hand away.

Mark walked back to Moriarty's car and got inside. He looked at the address Betty had given him. 347 Elm. He had no idea where Elm Street was, but how many streets could there be in downtown Brunton? He'd find this party goods store and take a look.

Nine

"So this novelty store was closed, of course, on a Sunday, but funny she thought to make that suggestion before I left." Mark filled in Detective Moriarty on his day's trip as they sat in Phebe's Sunday night, Mark nursing a red wine, Moriarty on his second Budweiser.

"So you think this Richard guy's driving around in a rubber mask running people over?"

"It doesn't sound particularly credible when you put like that, but there's a lot of money involved."

"This guy need money?"

"Not that I know of. He bought a new car and put a dent in it the first week."

"On purpose, says you."

"On purpose, says I."

"He buy it or the company buy it?"

Mark's eyebrows rose. "Good question. I didn't think to ask. I'll ask Betty when I talk to her." Mark pulled a small pad of paper from his back pocket and jotted down Moriarty's question.

"Real professional looking," said Moriarty.

"Saw it on *Columbo*," said Mark with a smile. "I'll forget if I don't write it down. You have to go home?"

Moriarty indicated his empty glass to a passing waiter, who picked it up it and continued on.

"Nope. My wife left."

"Visiting?"

"No. Left. As in gone. Good-bye. That's it. 'It's Over.' Roy Orbison. You heard of Roy Orbison?"

"Roy Orbison? Sure. I'm sorry to hear it," said Mark, sipping some wine in lieu of saying more.

"Not even an 'I'm Sorry.' That'd be Brenda Lee. How 'bout her?" Moriarty looked down. "Went off with some author. Nobody I ever heard of. Awakened her to aspects of life she never knew existed."

"Wow! Said she?"

"Said he, and she memorized it. She ain't that smart."

"Where'd she go?"

Moriarty gave a humorless laugh. "Living in the country with her 'awakener.' Cold Spring. Know where it is?"

"Yeah, up near Bear Mountain."

The waiter put a new beer on the table, and Moriarty took a long pull at it. "She's a frolicsome fifty-two years old. She needs awakening? Heh!"

Mark downed his wine "So how are you taking this?"

Moriarty tilted his glass back and forth and watched the beer slosh from side to side. "It's funny. There's something about her going off with some other guy grabs me the wrong way. Understand?"

"That I can understand."

"But now I get home, it's quiet. I don't have no deadline. There's no freaking agenda waiting for me. Nobody to answer to or have to entertain. All things considered, it's not so bad a trade-off, really."

"Do you have children?"

"One daughter, Beth. She's out in Los Angeles. I emailed her, and she called. She's a good kid. Always was. She's married herself with a little girl three years old. Cute as a button. So maybe she can understand a little. I don't know." Moriarty took a second long drink.

"I found this yellow thing, this yellow...pajama thing. See-through, no less."

"A negligee?"

Moriarty looked at him in bewilderment. "She didn't wear that stuff for me. I didn't even have to accuse her of anything. I asked about the...negligee, and she started spouting off. That's when she tossed off the 'aspects of life' thing. Imagine my fifty-two-year-old wife cavorting in a see-through yellow negligee." He spread his hands. "It boggles the mind."

Tony Babbitte entered the restaurant. When he saw Mark, he came over to the table and pulled out a chair. His arrival occasioned an abrupt change in topic.

"Mark," Tony began excitedly. "Can I borrow the *Richard Third* you promised?"

"Sure."

"Yeah. I...I...I'm not comfortable yet. It's eluding me."

Mark reflected on what he and Moriarty had attributed to Kristy's Richard. "Speaking of the Olivier, Tony, sometimes he tried to get a role down through disguise. A limp, a fake nose, or maybe some accent nailed the character for him. Why don't you experiment with how your Richard looks and sounds? A certain carriage or voice...something like that may do it for you. Study what Lord Larry did to himself, make-up-wise, for his Richard. Poke around and try different things. You still have plenty of time."

Tony nodded through Mark's suggestions. "I will. Good idea. I have this long mirror in my apartment, and I found this great Richard Third hat. I don't know whether I can get to character through haberdashery, but I know what you mean." Tony rose.

"I'll bring it to the theater tomorrow."

"Thanks. Thanks. Good. Sorry to have butted in." He walked off.

"What's he so excited about?" said Moriarty.

"He's the star of our coming play."

"The king that bumps off everyone in his way?"

"Yep."

Moriarty signaled for another beer.

"You want to eat?" asked Mark. "I get the actor's twenty-five per cent discount here."

"Why not? I don't cook much. My frolicsome fifty did all of that."

Mark had to laugh. "Might as well have a few more beers while you're at it."

Moriarty lifted his glass toward Mark in a toast. "I like how you think."

When Moriarty asked the waiter for a refill, Mark requested menus and ordered another glass of wine for himself.

~ * ~

Mark was due at the theater at eleven o'clock Monday morning. He lay in bed, debating whether to skip breakfast, when the ringing of his cell phone made the decision for him. He'd left his phone on the dining table the night before, so he had to get out of bed to answer it, and once up, he might as well stay up. Besides, after the wine he'd drunk with Moriarty the night before, a tall glass or two of orange juice would suit.

"Hello," said Mark. He looked between the security bars of his window at the bright July day outside. At the moment, the faint breeze coming into his apartment along with the sounds of a nearby siren and traffic seemed fresh, almost fragrant. A good day in the offing.

"Hello, is this Mark Louis?" A woman's voice.

"Yes."

"This is Betty King. I didn't know what time to call. I hope I haven't awakened you."

"No, I'm up and about to have breakfast. I have to be at the theater soon."

"I'm calling to tell you I visited the party store I told you about yesterday. I assume you went there, too."

"I did, but it was closed." He took a half gallon of orange juice from the refrigerator, shook it, and poured himself a glass.

"I went first thing this morning. I should tell you they do not sell rubber masks of any president now or at Halloween. So Richard could not have gotten one in Brunton. I hope I've been of some help to you."

Mark laughed.

Betty's voice acquired an edge. "Is something funny?"

"No, no. I'm surprised you're taking my theories seriously."

"It is you who take them seriously. I'm taking an interest only to dissolve your theories. They seem to trouble you so much."

Mark took his note pad from the top of his dresser. "May I ask you another question while I have your ear?"

"Another theory?"

"Sure. Help me dissolve it?"

"Happily."

Mark sat at his dining table. "The car Richard bought. His money or the company's?"

"The company's, of course."

"So, it didn't cost him anything, and he didn't lose anything by putting a dent into it."

There was silence for a moment. "Does that tell you something?"

"Well, only the obvious. I'd like to see what Kristy thinks of it. If she ever talks to me again."

"So, you've haven't heard from her yet?"

"No. I'll see her at the theater today."

"No, you won't. I spoke with her. She didn't think you needed her today, so she and her girlfriends decided to stay an extra night in Atlantic City."

"*I* didn't need her?"

"The theater, I mean."

"Atlantic City?"

"Richard invited her, but if it makes you feel any better, she insisted on her girlfriends going along."

"Great." Mark ran a finger along the moisture of his glass.

"Mark."

"Yes."

"I hope this call didn't sound...catty. I'm afraid it's come off a little bit that way, and I didn't mean it to. I only wanted to show you how wrong you are."

"No problem. I'm glad you called, and I really appreciate your throwing in the part about Kristy and Richard being off together in Atlantic City."

Betty laughed lightly. "Kristy's staying with her friends. Richard has his own room."

Betty's laugh somehow made Mark feel closer to her. He added something to what he'd told her already. "My point about the dent is this: if Richard used his new car to run down your son, the dent he put in it earlier would conveniently hide any dent caused by hitting your son. Since he didn't pay for the car, what would he care about any dent? And he didn't want to be driving the same car that nearly hit your daughter earlier. Small points admittedly, but points nonetheless."

"He'd asked me about a new car long before that."

"Planning ahead?"

After a brief silence, Betty said, "You're an annoying young man."

"I love your daughter."

"Making you doubly annoying."

"Because I'm not Richard?"

"Because you're not Richard."

Mark took a quick swallow of juice. "I'll be happy to share with you any more theories I develop, if you'd like to hear them."

"I'll be happy to keep you up-to-date on Richard's pursuit of Kristy, if you'd like to know."

The 'gotcha' in Betty's voice made Mark laugh lightly. "We sound like a 1940s movie."

"Don't we? Let's not foolishly drive anything unnecessary between us, Mark. I do want to hear from you."

"I understand."

"And about this call. Sorry for...well, sorry."

"Nothing to be sorry for. We'll keep in touch." He hung up.

Ten

Kristy did not show up at the theater, and Mark was glad he had known ahead of time why. A case of Rosemount Shiraz, the wine Richard had promised him, sat in the lobby. Mark looked for a note but found none. He checked to see whether Kristy had left any message, but no one had heard from her. The actors who'd auditioned successfully were notified. Tomorrow they would gather at the theater to read through the play for the first time. He, Tony, and Marty spent the day going through the play scene by scene and discussing how each should be played. After giving Tony the copy of Olivier's *Richard III*, Mark went home, a bottle of Richard's Shiraz under his arm, and as he walked, he wrestled with the question of whether to call Kristy. He picked up Chinese food again and after eating it, plopped into his one soft chair to let his mind drift from the wisdom of phoning Kristy to the staging of *Richard III* and back again. The deeper he got into his bottle of Shiraz, the more remote seemed the possibility of a call to Kristy. He'd done nothing to cause any guilt about not getting in touch with her. Besides, he'd already tried. Let her call him. Unfortunately, he could not restrain himself from poring over the six million possibilities of what Kristy was thinking; what Kristy was thinking he was thinking; what he was thinking Kristy was thinking. The pit seemed dizzying and bottomless. Alas, his one bottle of Shiraz wasn't. When he finished it, he walked down the street to a nearby watering hole, Meral's, and had a Black Label, the best Scotch the bar offered, while he continued to think about Kristy. Finally, stewed to the gills and unable to concentrate, he stumbled home and went to bed.

By eleven o'clock next morning, Mark had sufficiently rehydrated himself to the point where he could look forward to a day with Shakespeare. When he arrived at the theater, Kristy sat in the first row. She looked at him and smiled.

"What time do we read?" she said.

"When everyone gets here. It's called for eleven-thirty."

"You spoke to my mom."

"I did. She called yesterday."

"I mean you visited her."

Mark remained standing. "I did. She tell you about our conversation?"

"Yes. You have a certain persistence to you."

"I've been told it's one of my more charming qualities."

"Well, anyway, Atlantic City was me and my girlfriends." She looked down and then back up at him. "We were hardly with Richard the whole weekend. I don't want to make things worse than they are."

"And how bad are they?"

"You tell me."

Which way to go? "I don't know what you want me to say."

"What are you thinking?" Kristy's voice rose. "About me? About us?"

"I suppose I shouldn't say anything about your going off to Atlantic City with Richard."

"I told you. It was me, and Mary, and Laura. You've met them. Richard invited me to go with him alone, but no way I'd do that. I would go only if my girlfriends came along. He agreed and got us a big room, and we stayed together like we do in Chelsea. The three of us gambled a little, ate too much, went on the beach, and walked the boardwalk. We got to see Neil Sedaka."

"So now you know—breaking up is hard to do."

"Impossible, I hope."

They looked at one another in silence for a brief moment.

"Where was Richard while you were with the girls?" asked Mark.

"At the tables."

"He's a gambler?"

"He plays. Nothing big, he says. He gambles enough to get comped. It's how he got the two rooms."

"You stayed for free?"

"And ate for free and saw Neil Sedaka for free. Too good to pass up for me and my chaperones."

Mark laughed. "There's one thing better you could have taken along."

"You?"

"Me."

"Somehow, I don't think it would have worked out on this trip. Take me to dinner tonight?"

"Are you allowing me to forgive you?"

"Mark!"

Mark raised his hand. "I merely want to thank you for the opportunity." Mark enjoyed seeing Kristy's face soften into a smile. "Maybe a step or two up from Phebe's?"

"Yes, but my treat. I insist. After all, I had a free weekend." She lowered her voice. "And I'm a little rich girl you know now, so I'll take you. Can we go home and shower after work today and then go out for dinner?"

"Home? Ours?"

"Ours."

"Shower?"

"Among other things."

Mark walked to her and brushed the back of his hand across her cheek. Tears welled, but he didn't want Kristy to see *that*, so he cleared his throat and said, "I'll go downstairs to see whether we're ready."

"I'll wait here."

Mark leapt onto the stage and went downstairs to assemble the cast.

~ * ~

Showering after their day's work became an hour-and-a-half experience. When they were clean, mildly exhausted, and quite hungry, they found a cab, and Mark directed the driver to Giando's, a restaurant on the Brooklyn side of the Williamsburg Bridge. It was all windows and faced Manhattan. The downtown bridges, the South Street Seaport, and the classic forest scene of skyscrapers along with the East River comprised the view.

Earlier, back at his apartment, he'd offered Kristy the Brunton police report, but she refused to read it. "My mom told me." Mark let the subject drop.

"You'll enjoy the sunset from here," Mark promised as Mike, the *maître d'*, escorted them to a table. "Sit on this side. You'll see it better."

A tall, slim tuxedo-clad waiter, who introduced himself as Danny, delivered their menus, took their drink orders, and left.

"How did you find this place?" asked Kristy.

"I don't hear suspicion in your voice, do I?"

Kristy made a show of not condescending to answer such a question.

Mark laughed. "I read about it in the *Times* a while ago. You were off somewhere, and I was feeling sorry for myself. I took a cab and found it, sat at the bar and ate and talked to Tony, the bartender, and then Joey, the bartender, when the shift changed. Mike, the *maitre d'*, introduced himself. I liked it here. Felt homey. You *are* the first, and shall be the *only,* woman I ever bring here."

"I should hope so. I'm starving. Let's order."

Danny returned with their drinks.

"Don't leave," Mark said to him. "We'll order." After placing the order, Mark went on. "So, tell me. How much does Richard gamble? Could he owe the casino money?"

"Mark, you can't owe the casino money. You can't play with IOUs. Richard makes a good salary. He can afford what he does."

"I guess. What does he get for free?"

"At the casino? I told you. Rooms, food, shows."

"All for *free*?"

"I'm pretty sure. I know Mary and Laura and I didn't pay for anything. Oh, look."

The sun had set behind the downtown buildings, casting a pink aura across the sky.

"Were you here before when the sun set?"

Mark poked his thumb back over his shoulder. "At the bar."

Kristy reached across the table for Mark's hand. "And you thought of me. It's beautiful."

"Are you moving back in with me?' Mark asked softly.

"If you want me to. But please. Nothing more about Richard."

Mark looked into Kristy's eyes. "I'll do my best. What do you want to do Sunday?" Sunday was their next day off.

"Sunday, I have to go home." She released Mark's hand and sat back. "It's the anniversary of my father's death, and we're going to the cemetery."

"Oh. I didn't know. A year ago, eh?"

Kristy nodded.

"A car…" Mark caught himself but forced his conversation on. "… accident."

"Yes."

Kristy did not react to his hesitation, so he asked another question. "How did the accident happen?"

"He was driving along Route Eighteen, a pretty stretch alongside a hill about eight or ten miles outside of Brunton. Somehow, the car ended up going over the edge in one of those scenic rest areas."

"It wasn't struck by another car?"

"No."

"The car in good working order? Did they check afterward?"

"Nothing wrong with the car. So say the police."

"They have any idea how it happened?"

Kristy looked past Mark and out the window again. "There was no guard rail, only a curb, a grassy hill, and then a drop. They've put up a guard rail since."

"Where was he going?"

"To look at a possible store location in a nearby town, Haverford, to see whether it might be worth opening a second retail store."

"Terrible."

She returned her gaze to Mark. "It could have been worse. He originally planned to take Brian with him, but Brian got stuck at the warehouse trying to straighten out some order that got fouled up."

"Why didn't Richard go instead?"

"He was already waiting in Haverford. He'd found the site."

"Can I make the trip with you Sunday? I won't intrude on the visit to the cemetery, but I'd like to spend a little time in Brunton."

Kristy brightened. "That's sweet. Of course you can come. I'm renting a car again."

Their salads arrived, and while they ate, they discussed the sunset and each other. During any lull, Mark's mind drifted away to Brunton, Haverford, car accidents, and Richard.

Eleven

"My dad's stuff from his office is piled in the spare room, and the map you wanted is on the kitchen counter," said Kristy. "We're leaving now for the cemetery."

"We won't be long," Betty added. "I know you'll keep yourself busy theorizing."

The gentle tone of Betty's jibe took any possible sting out of it.

"Just trying to get a picture of things," Mark said from sofa in the living room. He returned Betty's gentle dig with one of his own. "Bringing Richard back with you?"

Betty ignored the remark and started for the door. Kristy responded. "No. We're picking him up and dropping him back home after."

Earlier, as they drove to Brunton, Mark had asked Kristy if he could go through her father's business effects. Kristy hadn't said no, and to Mark's surprise, Betty went along, even volunteering to pull out the Haverford documents for him when he mentioned they were of particular interest.

When the door closed behind the two women, Mark went into the kitchen and spread the local map out across the kitchen table.

Haverford was two towns southwest of Brunton. He found Route 18 and followed it with his finger back and forth between Brunton and Haverford. According to the map key, some thirteen miles separated the towns, with one town, Springfield, in between. The accident had occurred between Springfield and Haverford. Mark wanted to make the drive along Route 18 before Kristy got back. She and her mother had taken Betty's BMW, so the rented Chevrolet was his for the afternoon.

The spare room was on the third floor along with two other rooms: one an office, the other a guest bedroom. Betty said the current and pending business records were kept at the office behind the store in town. All the older other material had been moved to the spare room.

Mark started with the documents and letters from a law firm in Haverford to Mr. King discussing the size of the property and the terms of the lease. Mark wrote down the names and addresses of both the property and the law firm. Another letter indicated the time and place of the meeting that never took place. He looked through Mr. King's appointment book and found the date of his death and the notation "Haverford." Someone had crossed out "2:30," the time indicated in the letter, and written "1:30" above it. Mark made a mental note of the change and set out for Haverford.

He found the rest area between Springfield and Haverford, where the accident occurred, and pulled in. He drove through it slowly and saw how, without the guard rail in place, a quick spurt of acceleration could send a car sailing. He noticed, off to the side, a dark area of thickly clustered trees—the high school lovers' lane Kristy had once teased him about. The image of Richard and her cuddling there on warm, summer nights hurried him along, and he exited the rest area more speedily than safely. From there to the outskirts of Haverford, the road twisted alongside a precipitous incline lined with a low, metal barrier made of one wide, horizontal slat.

He found the Haverford address easily—158 Main Street—a corner property with a store downstairs—and what looked like an apartment above. He noticed a sign in the apartment window. Mark parked the car and looked more closely at the sign. "Apartment For Rent. Two bedrooms—partially furnished—seven hundred fifty dollars a month." His own rattrap of a no-bedroom apartment cost him twelve hundred dollars a month. The store had been leased to a nail salon—one of the few Main Street businesses open on a Sunday. One young woman sat behind a counter staring at her phone as another young woman worked on an older lady's nails. He went inside.

"Excuse me," he said to the woman behind the counter. "I wonder if there's some way I can get a phone number."

"For?" She sounded bored and looked bored.

"A law firm, Rogers and Robinson. I have their office number, but I'm sure no one's there on a Sunday. Is there a local paper they advertise in? Maybe an emergency number or a cell number?"

She pointed behind Mark's head to a bulletin board covered with business cards and notices. "Maybe there."

"Oh, I didn't notice it. Thanks." Mark looked the board over but found nothing from Rogers and Robinson. He thought of Mr. Gehring, Ashley's lawyer, but couldn't imagine any use he could put him to at the moment. He would certainly not have the phone number of a lawyer from Haverford, Pennsylvania. "No, nothing. Thanks." He left the store.

Mark wanted to ask the lawyers about the change in the time of the meeting, but now it would have to wait until a Monday phone call. A police car drove by, went half a block, and pulled up to a very municipal looking building. Mark walked that way and stopped in front of a brick building with "City Hall" carved in brown stone above the door. A phone book emergency? Why not?

He entered the building and followed the "Police" signs. The officer at the desk looked him over. "Help you?"

"Yeah, maybe. I'm trying to get a phone number of someone in Haverford. Is there a local phone book? I'd've gone to the library if it wasn't a Sunday."

"Sure. Got one right here." The officer bent and pulled up a small phone book. The front pages were white, the back were yellow.

"That's not just for Haverford, is it?" asked Mark.

"No, Haverford and hereabouts."

"Thanks." Mark took the book over to a wooden chair and flipped through the pages to the R's. He found two Rogerses, one with the proper initial, and three Robinsons, none of whom had the proper initial. After jotting down the one number, he handed the book back and expressed his gratitude. He went outside and dialed John Rogers on his cell.

"Hello."

"I'm looking for John Rogers, the lawyer."

"You've found him. Who's calling, please?"

"My name is Mark Louis, and I'm a friend of the King family."

"From Brunton?"

"Yes, sir."

"What can I do for you?"

The lawyer's voice remained eager and friendly, not, it seemed, annoyed by a Sunday call. Honesty might be worth the effort.

"I'm living with Kristy in New York, although I happen to be in Haverford today. Kristy and her mother are visiting the cemetery right now. It's been a year since the accident."

"Oh, yes. Is it one year already? I knew Mr. King pretty well. Very sad event. Kristy's trying her hand at acting now, I hear?"

"Yes, sir. She and I met in the acting community in New York City, and we work together now."

"Nice young lady. I believe I asked what I could do for you."

"I'm interested in something Kristy mentioned about the day her father died." A small divergence from the truth wouldn't hurt. "She said the time of the meeting in Haverford was changed from two-thirty to one-thirty. You were supposed to be at the meeting, too, I understand?"

There was silence for a moment. "Yes, I was waiting in Haverford, but I don't remember the time of the meeting being changed."

"I wonder. Do you have your calendar from last year at home with you?"

"I suppose I do..." Reluctance crept into the lawyer's voice, so Mark spoke up quickly. "Can you check on the time? I can call you back in, say, fifteen minutes. That's the only thing I really wanted to know, whether the meeting time was altered. The family would appreciate it, I'm sure." Mark held his breath.

"Well, yes. Fifteen minutes then."

Mark toured Main Street, and fifteen minutes later John Rogers told him that according to his calendar, the two-thirty meeting had not been rescheduled.

"Thanks," said Mark. "I didn't think so. You've been very helpful." He got back into the rented Chevy and returned to Brunton. Now, he had another oddity to deal with—an unaccounted hour on the day Kristy's father died. Time enough for Richard to somehow cause Mr. King's auto accident before driving innocently to Haverford and make the original meeting time of two-thirty. Mark wished he could have peppered John Rogers with more questions, but he knew he'd been lucky to get this one question answered. Betty would have to be the one to do any peppering of the lawyer if he could bring himself to tell her his added suspicions—and if she believed him.

Mark pulled into the King driveway. Raising the issue of the time discrepancy would cause another explosion with Kristy, but he couldn't turn aside. The trail not only led him on but pulled him forward. He was in its grasp, and a hair-raising conversation with Betty King loomed as the next dubious treat along the way.

Twelve

"So, what are you afraid of?" Detective Moriarty asked before he took a long swig from his glass of beer.

Mark laughed. "Afraid? Me? Why should I be afraid? I need to tell Kristy's mom that, in my estimation, her son-in-law of choice used an hour's discrepancy no one seems to know about to see to it her husband's car went over a cliff. I've already told her Richard probably murdered her son and tried to kill her daughter. She somewhat doubts the truth of my claims. Not to mention, Kristy has left me once, partly because of my suspicions and has only recently returned."

"So tell her anyway," said Moriarty. "Your girlfriend gets mad and leaves, how bad could it be? You lived through it once, and here you are." He shrugged and drained his glass. "There are other women."

Mark rolled his eyes. "I don't think you're the one to cheer me on in this case."

"Heh, probably not."

He and Kristy had been back together since their sunset dinner, but Kristy was spending this Monday night in her Chelsea apartment, as she often did, doing laundry, paying bills. "Getting organized," she called it. Mark had no opportunity to speak with Betty on Sunday after the cemetery visit and couldn't find the courage to call her any time afterward. He'd called Moriarty instead and invited him to meet in Phebe's after work. "But you have to tell her," Moriarty insisted. "The mother, I mean. She has to check for herself. The lawyer you tracked down in Haverford will talk more freely to her than to you. She'll figure it out you give her a chance. You said she's open-minded."

"If I were sure she wouldn't flip out...but I'm not. She'd might get pissed, tell Kristy, and I'll be alone again."

Moriarty shrugged. He did a lot of shrugging lately. "Alone ain't so bad."

"Yeah, well. Kristy's better." Mark tapped his empty wineglass impatiently on the tabletop. "I'm going to call Betty. If I don't do it now, Kristy'll be back tomorrow night, and I might not find a chance. You mind if I step outside?"

The waiter placed another beer in front of Moriarty. "Just don't take my beer with you."

"I won't. Wish me luck."

Moriarty lifted his glass an inch off the table.

Mark walked out onto the sidewalk and placed the call.

"Hello?"

Tension flashed through his stomach. "Hi, Betty?"

"Mark?"

"Yes."

"How are you?"

"Better than I expect to be in a few minutes."

"Oh? Now what?"

"Let me tell you what I have to. Please don't interrupt."

"Go on." An edge crept into Betty's voice, but there was no going back. He explained how he'd found an hour's discrepancy in the original time of the meeting on the day of her husband's death, and the time rewritten in her husband's calendar. He reported on his talk with the Haverford lawyer.

"This is an unaccounted-for hour on the day your husband died. Someone changed the meeting time for him. You can see the crossing out in his book. The change got your husband on the road an hour earlier than originally planned. Someone changed the meeting time on his end, but not the Haverford end. Someone wanted him available for an hour before the meeting."

A crowded bus went by as he plowed on. "Rogers, the lawyer, says he didn't change the time. I suspect Richard did. Then, when he called your husband to change the meeting time, he also arranged to meet him along the road—in the rest area. He may have suggested they talk once more before they met the lawyers. I think Richard put the missing hour to use. He did what he had to do at the rest area, then arrived for the meeting in Haverford at the regular time and waited, along with everyone else, for your husband. I believe it was his first move in trying to worm his way into control of your business. I can't understand why yet. According to you, he's treated very well. And... and that's what I wanted to tell you."

"Couldn't my husband have penciled in an earlier meeting with someone else at one-thirty? A short meeting would still give him time to get to Haverford? Did you ever consider that?"

The iciness of Betty's tone increased.

"Well, no. Two-thirty was crossed out and one-thirty written above it. It was clearly a time change." Mark waited. "Hello? Hello, Betty, are you still there?"

"I am. Are you quite finished?"

"Yes." A small dog stopped to sniff at Mark's leg, and the elderly lady walking the dog gave a tug on the leash. Mark took a step to the left and frowned at the woman.

Betty's voice refocused him. "Would you like my reaction?"

"Very much," he answered.

"Here it is." The connection cut off immediately, and Mark stood still, holding the phone stupidly to his ear.

"Betty?" he said softly, but the call was over. He went back inside Phebe's.

"How'd it go?" asked Moriarty. A fresh glass of wine awaited Mark.

"She hung up on me."

"Oh, sorry. Before or after?"

"After I told her my story."

"You accomplished something, then."

Mark took his seat and sipped his wine. "What I accomplished was probably to make a mountain of trouble for myself. She's going to tell Kristy. I know she is. I know she is," he finished softly.

"Why don't you tell her first?"

Mark took a second sip of wine. "Because there's a chance she *won't* tell Kristy, I guess. Thanks for the wine, by the way." He'd need it and a few glasses more before the night was over.

Thirteen

"Why do you keep asking me about my mother? And what's been wrong with you this week?"

Mark and Kristy lay in bed the following Saturday, not due at the theater until noon. Mark had heard nothing from Betty and nothing from Kristy about Betty. He didn't know whether the week's safe passage meant Betty had chosen to keep the conversation between the two of them private or whether the passage of time made the revelation to Kristy more imminent.

Mark swatted the topic away and moved on to the coming play. "*Richard's* starting to round into shape, and it better round into shape."

Kristy draped an arm across Mark's stomach. "We had an acceptable walk-through yesterday. Tony's looking good. He didn't think so, as usual, but we both know he'll be terrific."

"If he calms down."

"Nothing else on your mind?"

Mark kissed Kristy on the forehead. "Nothing more than that. Now, love me." He nestled deeper and buried his head on her shoulder.

"Don't you mean 'Make love to me'?"

He looked at her. "I mean that, too, yes." He ran his hand up and down her body, but the ring of the phone interrupted. "Let it ring," he mumbled.

"It might be the theater. You better take it."

Mark reached across Kristy and picked up the receiver. The voice on the other end sent a cannonball into his stomach.

"Good morning, Mark. This is Betty. I hoped to catch you before you left for the theater. Is Kristy there?"

"Yes, right here." He handed the phone to Kristy and watched her face. He hadn't detected any threat in Betty's voice, but fear had turned his mind to jelly.

"I can't come tomorrow, Mom. Our next day off is Tuesday." She looked at Mark for confirmation. He nodded.

"How about if we come down Monday evening? No, I think we better eat dinner here and let traffic clear out. We'll be there maybe nine-thirty, ten. Good. Of course, he'll come. Bye."

"Your mother?"

"You know it was my mother. She wants us to visit."

"She say why?"

"Nope, but I'm glad she invited us. Maybe she's getting used to me being here doing what I do and understanding that my interest in liquor is limited to the wine I share with you." She cozied back next to Mark. "Now, where were we?"

Mark had lost the moment—the phone call had withered it—and his performance paled in contrast to Kristy's desire. The beginning of the end, he warned himself. Get ready for it.

~ * ~

Among this princely heap, if any here
By false intelligence, or wrong surmise,
Hold me a foe;
If I unwillingly, or in my rage,
Have aught committed that is hardly borne
To any in this presence, I desire
To reconcile me to his friendly peace:
'Tis death to me to be at enmity;
I hate it, and desire all good men's love.

Barbara Gray, AWB business manager, appeared from backstage and stopped to listen.

I do not know that Englishman alive
With whom my soul is any jot at odds
More than the infant that is born to-night:
I thank God for my humility.

She stepped forward as soon as Tony finished his speech. Tony came downstage and looked at Mark, who sat alone in the third row.

"What do you think?" asked Tony.

Mark rose. "Tony, if we had a camera and I filmed what you're doing, you'd see how absolutely right you are, and how right you look."

"Is it right, you think? I did what you suggested." Tony stepped down from the stage and knelt in a first row seat, facing Mark. "This does help." He patted himself, indicating his clothing. He'd already shown Mark how he planned to begin the first act dressed in dreary, black Elizabethan tights with muted red trim and, after the wooing scene with Lady Anne, reverse the pattern and wear a more lavish red outfit with black trim.

"Olivier changes his clothes after the scene with the grieving widow," said Tony. "And red, you know, blood, violence. I feel great when I come back onstage dressed like that. It's a celebration of Richard knowing his plan to murder and marry his way to the crown will work."

"Great idea, Tony. Works like a charm. Go rest a while. We're going to start soon. You'll be worn out before we even begin."

Laughing, Tony leapt back onto the stage mumbling his lines and passed Barbara, a middle-aged, empty-nest housewife and former English major, who'd made AWB Rep her home and family. She eased herself down from the stage. Mark rose and waited for her.

"Hello, Mark. Tony's in heaven, isn't he?"

"He'll have a stroke if we don't get this play open soon."

"Exactly my question. A date for the opening?"

"Let me talk to Tony. I'll let you know. I know you need time to get the news out."

She took a step but then stopped. "Oh, you got another case of wine today. I had it put in the office."

"Another one?"

"The Australian wine. You gave me a bottle last time. Good stuff. Kristy's friend sent it, according to the card attached." She lifted her two hands in innocence. "I didn't snoop. The card's not in an envelope."

"No, no. I didn't think you did. I'm surprised is all."

"And there was a call for you. A prospective contributor, he said."

"How's anyone know we're looking for contributions?"

"Beats me, but here's the information." She handed him the index card. It read "Wallace," and listed a phone number.

"Wallace? First name or last?"

"First, I think. He said to have you call this number and ask for Wallace."

"I'll do it now while everyone is 'tiring."

"'Tiring. How very Elizabethan." They shared a laugh.

"Tell everybody twenty minutes."

"Will do." Mark helped Barbara back onto the stage. He walked up the aisle to the office, where he sat on the one chair the tiny office held and punched in the '718' number.

A male voice with a disinterested edge to it said, "Hello?"

"I'd like to speak to Wallace, please."

"Moment."

"Hello," came a different voice.

"This is Mark Louis of AWB Theatre Company. Is this Wallace?"

"Ah, yes. I'm glad you called back."

"I had a message you called earlier."

"I represent someone interested in making a substantial contribution to your theater group."

"Well, I have to admit I'm surprised. We haven't actively solicited contributions, but a contribution is always welcome. Who's our benefactor?"

"He says to tell you he's a friend. Can we leave it at that?"

"A friend of yours or ours?"

"Mutual, it would seem." Wallace gave a stilted laugh.

"I'd still like to know the name of this friend."

"He wants to be anonymous at this time."

A growing tension centered Mark's concentration. "What kind of a contribution does he have in mind?"

"Let me say substantial."

"Wallace or Mr. Wallace. You won't tell me how much this person would like to contribute, and you won't tell me who's making the contribution?"

A less friendly pall descended on the line. "Mr. Louis, I think for the moment all you really need to know is a five-figure contribution is available to your theater company. We can discuss specifics later. I need to know whether you're interested."

He'd either be crazy to follow up on this too-mysterious Wallace character or crazy for *not* following up with so much money at stake, but he had no need to make a firm decision yet. Maybe he could find out more about this Wallace by checking the phone number with Moriarty. "Well, sure I'm interested."

"Good. I'll talk with my client then."

"And should I call you back?"

"Yes, you can."

"A day or two?"

"That'll be fine."

The connection broke.

Fourteen

Had anyone ever sat blithely in a rental car and driven himself to his own execution, Mark wondered, as he slowed to negotiate a curve in the road? Rehearsals had run long on Monday, so he and Kristy put off their departure for Brunton until Tuesday morning. He hadn't tried to wriggle out of this trip, nor had he contemplated telling Kristy he had an additional reason to believe Richard a murderer. Instead, he drove on, a passive prisoner on whom a malevolent fate waited to cast its woeful verdict.

How would he get home after Kristy's imminent and inevitable blow up?

"Does Brunton have bus service to New York?" he asked.

"There's a small Greyhound office at the edge of town. We'll pass it on the way in. Why?"

"Just wondering how isolated Brunton is."

Kristy closed her eyes again, and Mark drove on.

As soon as they arrived at the King house, Betty put cold cuts and rye bread on the kitchen table for them. It was a beautiful second day of August, hot but with a breeze that made the yellow kitchen curtains dance. The two women talked as Mark ate and kept a sly eye on them. He hoped Betty hadn't planned a public execution for him. If the guillotine were to drop, he hoped Betty would do it out of his presence. Kristy would come back, stony-faced and disappointed in him and know why he'd asked the location of the bus station.

He got his answer when Betty said, "Mark, do you mind if I take Kristy for a walk? I want to talk to her." Mark pulled in a deep breath and said, "No, I don't mind at all. I brought a book with me. It's in the car, or maybe I'll take a walk myself." He pushed himself away from the kitchen table and went outside. He took *The Three Coffins*, a 1935 murder mystery by John Dickson Carr, from the floor of the car where he'd tossed it, slid it into the back pocket of his jeans, and started to walk.

The house was empty when he returned an hour later. He eyed the bar in the living room and found the inviting Chivas bottle behind it but reconsidered. If he had to face Kristy's anger, a clear head would at least allow him to duck more efficiently. He slumped onto the thickly cushioned, flowered chair and put his legs up on the matching ottoman. He adjusted himself to catch the light and tried to read.

It wasn't long before the kitchen door slammed, and Kristy's exasperated voice reached him.

"Mother!"

"It's what we both need," Betty's voice responded.

Kristy walked into the living room and threw herself onto the sofa. Her mother walked sedately to the bar.

"Mom, you are perfectly capable of running the company now and for as long as you want. My not wanting to have anything to do—"

Betty interrupted. "You had your opportunity to be involved with the company and with Richard"—she politely lowered her voice when she said Richard—"but you didn't want either. I trust him, and I want him in control of the company."

"But you can't just give it to him."

"I'm not *just* giving it to him."

Mark considered stepping out of the room, but Betty's next sentence changed his mind.

"I'm giving him control only if I'm no longer around, and I plan to *be* around a good long time yet. Your interests are protected. Your income is protected. What would happen to the company and to you otherwise? Say, if Richard left and found another job?"

"I don't care about income, the company, or Richard. I care about you."

"Thank you," said Betty, "but you need not care about those other things because they've always been taken care of for you."

The women stewed for a moment until Kristy said, "Mom, I want you to change your mind."

"It's not your decision to make, darling. I have to do what I think is best for both of us."

"This is not going to make me think any differently about Richard. I don't care if you went to school with his father, and his grandfather took you to the zoo. Maybe you're partial to the name Richard, but this Richard is not for me. We tried. It didn't work. I didn't like it. The divorce will become final next month. Nothing will stop it. Giving everything away to Richard is some cheap...cheap stratagem you think will change how I feel."

"Kristy, you're becoming disrespectful—and irrational. I'm giving nothing away, and this has nothing to do with changing anything about you."

"You said since I'm not going to stay married to Richard, you had some changes to make. You pressured me before into doing something I didn't want to do, and you're pressuring me now when I want it even less. This is a cheap trick. A cheap, cheap trick. You're harming yourself to spite me and hoping I'll do something to save you from yourself."

"No, Kristy. This is about the company, security, and your welfare."

"I can look after my own welfare." Kristy rose, and Mark saw the tears in her eyes. "I can't stay here any longer and argue with you."

Betty did not reply. Her eyes shimmered as well. It was not a pretty scene.

Kristy said, "Come on, Mark."

"Are you leaving?" asked Betty.

"There's no point in staying. No point at all."

Betty's gaze fell to the floor. "I see."

Mark rose and started after Kristy, who had already stepped quickly from the living room into the kitchen. He paused to address Betty. "I'm sorry."

Betty managed a small smile and a nod of her head.

The kitchen door banged, and Mark hurried to catch up.

He gave Kristy five miles of quiet driving to decompress before he asked, "Can you tell me what happened back there? What did she do? Put Richard the Turd's name on all the company papers?"

"You're not funny."

He waited a decent interval and tried again. "Did she really sign the company over to him in her will?"

"Did she really? Did she really? Weren't you there? She must really hate you."

"Me!"

"Yes. To try to goad me into accepting Richard with her new will."

"Does Richard know yet?"

"No."

"So when will he know?"

"When she tells him."

"Hmm, why didn't I think of that?"

"I told you. You're *not* funny."

Mark let another five miles pass. "What exactly did she do?"

"I don't want to talk about it. Please."

Mark gave up and drove his silent way north, back to New York City.

~ * ~

A shaft of light slashed down the center aisle almost reaching the stage where Tony's Richard Third held forth. Mark sat in his accustomed third row seat, prepared, as always, to compliment Tony's performance and bolster his confidence. Tony paused at the interruption and pointed up the aisle. Mark saw Moriarty settling into a back-row seat. Moriarty waved, indicating rehearsal should continue.

"Where was I?" asked Tony.

Mark prompted, and Tony carried on.

Look, what is done cannot be now amended:
Men shall deal unadvisedly sometimes,
Which after-hours gives leisure to repent.
If I did take the kingdom from your sons,
To make amends I'll give it to your daughter.
If I have kill'd the issue of your womb,
To quicken your increase, I will beget
Mine issue of your blood upon your daughter;
A grandam's name is little less in love
Than is the doting title of a mother;
They are as children as one step below,
Even of your mettle, of your very blood.

Tony glanced at Mark and continued to the end of the speech.

Mark applauded. "Better and better, Tony."

Tony brought his hands together in one mammoth clap. "I think I'm getting it. I do, I do." He leapt down from the stage. "It's taking me over, Mark. I recite Richard in the shower, walking to the theater, eating, lying in bed. Let's schedule opening night and get this show on the road."

"How's two-and-a-half weeks? Time enough for publicity if we get Barbara on it right away. A mailing to subscribers. Notices in the weekly papers and the Off-Off list in the Sunday *Times*."

"Let's do it. I'm ready."

"I'll tell Barbara today."

"We go through Acts One and Two today?"

"Yes. In about an hour. Go rest. Save your voice."

"Tea, lemon, and honey for me. See you in an hour." He jumped back onto the stage and headed for the dressing room downstairs.

Mark walked to the back of the theater and sat across the aisle from Moriarty. "What's up, Detective?"

"Interesting friends you have."

"Tony?"

"Wallace."

"Oh. You found out something. Who is he?"

"Works for a fellow named Lowenstein."

Mark shook his head.

"Big name in gambling."

"Gambling!"

"Yeah. Your benefactor comes from the wrong side of the tracks, and he's got no particular history of giving money away."

Mark stood and faced Moriarty. "If he *is* my benefactor. Why's he being so generous, you think?"

"You tell me."

"I can't."

"You said your friend Richard is a gambler?"

"Kristy says he is. Atlantic City. Nothing big, according to her."

"Might be some connection?"

Why would a gambler unknown to him be offering him money? He stood up straight. "Richard sent me a second case of wine. Did I tell you?"

"You didn't. Oh, I see where you're going. I wonder if your lady friend told him you think he's a murderer."

"I doubt very much she'd do that."

"Think he got wind of your opinion somehow?"

"I don't see how, but certainly not from Kristy."

"He's being awful nice to you. Especially if he's hooked up with this Lowenstein."

"You think he's trying to buy me off? If he is, it's an admission of guilt."

Moriarty waffled his right hand. "That's a big jump. Admission to you maybe, not to nobody else. Not to me."

"So what do you think I should do now?"

"I think you might as well follow this Lowenstein thing through. At least call your Wallace contact again. See what he says."

"He didn't mention Richard's name in connection with the donation."

"Maybe Richard wants to make sure you're open to suggestion before he attaches his name to a friendly bribe. If it *is* a bribe, you can bet he won't want to remain anonymous for long."

"You're right about that. He'll want credit. Otherwise, there's no point to it. I haven't told you yet what Kristy says her mother's doing."

"Tell me now."

"It wasn't easy to get out of her. I had to *pry* it out, but she says her mother isn't giving Richard a big raise after all."

"My heart aches."

"But if she dies, he gets enough of her share of the company to give him control. Fifty-one per cent. Kristy gets the rest."

Moriarty scratched at his right ear. "Sounds like she's asking for trouble, don't it? I mean flat out asking. Assuming your theory holds water."

"Kristy thinks it's her mom's way of pressuring her to stay married to Richard. I don't know. Betty must have called John Rogers, the lawyer in Haverford, to confirm what I told her about the change of meeting time. She *must* have."

"Why don't you call him again and ask whether he's heard from her."

Mark glanced at his watch. "No time like the present. I'm deep enough in, it can't hurt, I guess."

"I'll wait here."

Mark went into the small lobby and entered the office. Barbara sat at the desk.

"Barbara, let's set an opening date of Thursday, two plus weeks from now. We can get in two weeks before Labor Day, give ourselves a long weekend, and run it into October. Extend it, even, if it does well."

Barbara checked the large wall calendar over her left shoulder. "The nineteenth?"

Mark eyed the calendar and agreed. "You know what to do. A mailing, the newspapers."

"I know. I'll get right on it."

"I need the office for a few minutes. A private phone call."

Barbara stood. "It's time for a break, anyway."

Mark called the lawyer's phone on his cell. "John Rogers, please. Tell him Mark Louis is calling, and it's very important."

A minute and a half went by. "Hello, this is John Rogers."

"Mr. Rogers, this is Mark Louis. I spoke to you about a possible discrepancy in the meeting time last year when Mr. King was killed in the car accident."

"Yes, I recall."

"Mrs. King asked me to call and thank you again for your help."

"Oh, she thanked me enough when I spoke with her."

Too easy. "And you confirmed for her the meeting time not being changed on your end?"

"Yes, and I told the same thing to Mr. Sutor when he called. So I hope it clears up any misunderstanding about the day."

Hearing Richard's name sent a chill through Mark. "Mr. Sutor called you, too, right?"

"Yes."

"Do you remember whether he called you before or after Mrs. King?"

"The day after her, as a matter of fact. He seemed surprised when I told him you had asked about the meeting, too."

Ah, there it was. "You told him I spoke with you?"

"Oh, yes. I want to be perfectly frank with everyone. I'm not about to have my credibility or reputation questioned, especially in connection with something like this, where the poor man lost his life."

"No, I don't blame you. You did the right thing. Thanks for your time."

Mark returned to Moriarty. "Not only did Betty call the lawyer, but so did Richard. Betty must have asked Richard about the time of the meeting and maybe even brought up the lawyer's name. At any rate, Richard called the lawyer the day after Betty did, and the lawyer told him I'd called about the meeting time, so he knows I'm sniffing around."

"And then comes the offer from Wallace."

"And the second case of wine, for whatever *that's* worth." Mark leaned on the back of the seat two rows in front of Moriarty.

"Heh! Poor lawyer's gonna wonder why everybody's in heat over this meeting time."

"Forget about the lawyer. Listen, I'll call Wallace and set up a meeting. You'll be around to help, I trust?"

"'Backup' is the term you're looking for. I'll be your backup with more available if necessary."

"Good. We'll talk after I've set it up."

Moriarty got to his feet. "I gotta go. Meet me for a drink later?"

"Six at Phebe's?"

"Make it seven."

"I'll be there."

Fifteen

Moriarty walked into Phebe's at seven-fifteen, and Mark waved him over to his table, where he hung his jacket over the back of a chair and sat. They ordered drinks, a beer for Moriarty and a red wine, Mark's second, and made small talk until the drinks arrived. Mark told about his call to Wallace. "He doesn't want to meet, and he sounded awfully impatient."

"He mention any names?"

"No, he said someone would be in touch soon."

"With you?"

"That's what he said."

Moriarty took off his tie, folded it, and jammed it into his inside jacket pocket. "Your girlfriend coming?"

"Yeah, she'll be here in a little while."

"I won't stay then. One beer and home. I'm tired anyway."

"So what should I do about this Wallace character?"

"If *he's* gonna contact *you*, don't do nothing. Let me know if the call comes. Meanwhile, maybe *I'll* do something."

"Like what?"

"Maybe this Wallace or one of his associates will get a parking ticket or a summons he'll have to explain in the precinct. I can arrange to meet him. Maybe apply some pressure."

Moriarty's heavy-handed suggestion surprised Mark. "Whatever you think."

Moriarty drained his glass and stood. "I'm off. Keep in touch." He put his jacket on and left.

Mark nursed his red wine—he didn't want to be sailing on three glasses of wine when Kristy arrived—trying to sort things out. Kristy arrived half an hour later.

"Glad to see you," said Mark. "I've been nursing this one glass long enough. Hungry?"

Kristy kissed Mark and sat next to him. "Sure am, but I can't."

"Why not?"

"Richard called me. He wants to meet tonight."

Mark frowned. "He's in the city then?"

"He is."

"Where's he staying?"

"The Millenium. Downtown."

"Church Street. I know where it is. So, you're going?"

"I said no, but he insisted. He wants to buy us dinner."

"Us?"

"Us. Me and you. He said he has something for you. He thinks you know what it is already."

"He said that?"

"Yes. What is it?"

Mark told her the story of Wallace and the mysterious contribution. He omitted Moriarty's report of a gambling connection or his own suspicions of a bribe.

"You think Richard's behind this contribution?" Kristy sounded perplexed. "Why would Richard want to make such a big contribution? *Five* figures, he said?"

"This guy Wallace said."

"Why wouldn't Richard make the contribution openly?"

"To impress you?"

Kristy scoffed at the suggestion.

Mark toyed for a moment with telling Kristy about Lowenstein and the gambling, but didn't want to take a chance of making her either angry or defensive again.

"So is Richard meeting us here?" said Mark.

"I told him we'd meet him at the bar in the Millenium."

"When?"

"Nine. But I need a snack. I'm famished."

Mark handed Kristy the menu. "Does Richard know about your mother's new will?"

"He does," Kristy answered as she glanced over the menu.

"How'd he react?"

She lowered the menu. "He's pleased my mother has so much confidence in him, and he wishes he could share his good fortune with me."

"Got to admire his single-trackedness."

"*Their* single-trackedness. Let's not talk about Richard. Let's not think about him until we have to. I can inform you I'm available for carnal activity again."

"Does an upswing in mood go along with that?"

"Have I been…?"

"No need for an adjective, darling. This whole week's been unsettled since our visit to your mom's."

"Life goes on. A plate of calamari suit you?"

"It does."

"Then, let's get some."

"And so we shall."

~ * ~

"I'm really getting up in the world," said Mark when he stepped off the elevator at the second floor. He took a few steps and turned right into the Millenium's small, dark, expensive-looking bar. Mark took Kristy's elbow and led her inside. "The bar stools are upholstered and have backs to them. I don't know whether I can stand the opulence. Nice looking restaurant." The hotel restaurant operated next to the bar.

"Oh, be quiet," said Kristy. "Sit. You've been places like this before."

Mark helped Kristy to a seat.

"Oh, a gentleman even."

"Even? Not even. As *always*. I hope friend Richard treats tonight. Wine's got to be at least fifteen bucks a glass here, more than I pay for a whole *bottle*—a *big* bottle."

"He'll pay, don't worry. I'm surprised he's not here already. Oh, there he is." She nodded toward the bar entrance.

Mark's stomach whirled—jealousy?—when he caught sight of Richard, nattily dressed, as usual. Richard's eyes found Kristy, and he smiled as he approached. Mark stood, and the two men shook hands.

"I'm glad you could make it," said Richard, settling onto the bar seat next to Kristy. "Ah, no glasses in front of you, so you've only now arrived." He leaned forward to look past Kristy and gave a Mark friendly smile. "Pretty good detective myself, eh? Let's have a drink before we eat." He motioned for the bartender.

"What brings you to New York?" asked Mark, ignoring the detective remark but puzzled by it.

"Business. Always business." He spoke for a few moments about his day. "Did your case of Shiraz arrive okay?"

"Oh, yes," said Mark. "I should have thanked you earlier. Two cases is very generous. You'll make me feel like a freeloader."

Richard waved off the need for gratitude. "There's plenty where that came from."

Kristy asked, "Is the wine what you meant when you said Mark knew what you had for him?"

"No, no. I want to do something for the theater. For you." He tapped Kristy's arm.

Mark worked on his wine and listened to Richard's spiel about how helpful he wanted to be. As he listened, he wondered what, if anything, Kristy or her mother had mentioned about his suspicions of Richard *to* Richard. If the gifts to the theater were an attempt at ingratiating himself, it could only have stemmed from the two women talking to him or the one conversation he had with John Rogers, the lawyer.

When Richard slowed down, Mark asked, "Who is this Wallace who called?"

"He's involved in some business I'm doing. I work a lot with him."

"Is he donating, too?"

"No, no. But he...I do...he's involved in some business things with me. Sort of like an agent. You know."

Richard redirected his conversation toward Kristy again, and Mark fell back into his reveries. Soon, Mark heard his name and returned his attention to his host.

The wine cost twelve dollars a glass, but since they'd each had only one, Mark offered to pick up the tab. Richard wouldn't hear of it, and Mark surrendered quickly. When Richard slid his money from his right pants pocket to pay the bar bill, a small ticket fell to the floor. Kristy bent to pick it up, and Mark noticed the word Resorts on it. Kristy noticed it too, because she said, "You were in Atlantic City again?"

"I drove down for a couple hours." He flashed a big grin at Kristy. "Life was easier when OTB was still in business." He threw two twenties on the table and returned his gaze to Mark. "Oh, and someone will be in touch regarding the donation."

"Well, I'm sure Kristy appreciates your kindness as much as I do," Mark said, offering an accommodating grin, which left a bad taste in his mouth. The *maître d'* led them to a table, and a quiet dinner followed.

Afterward, everyone rode down the escalator and said good-bye. Mark and Kristy went out onto Church Street, and Richard returned to his room.

"Since I saved thirty dollars tonight, I'll get us a cab home," said Mark.

One quickly appeared, and he and Kristy settled inside.

"Two questions, darling," said Mark.

"Yes, precious?"

"Did you or your mother ever pass along to Richard anything I discussed about him with you?"

"Of course not. Well, certainly not me. No. I'm sure my mother wouldn't either."

"He doesn't know what I think of him?"

"Not from me."

"Nothing at all?"

"He knows you are the man I love. He knows we live together. He knows you are responsible for two murders being solved. I did brag a little to him about you."

"Oh, so that was the reason for the detective remark tonight. He knows I was involved in solving those two murders?"

"Yes."

"But nothing about my suspicions of him?"

"Stop already. No. How could I tell him that?"

"Does he know about Moriarty?"

Kristy yawned and leaned her head on Mark's shoulder. "What about Moriarty?"

"That he's a cop. That he got the accident report from the Brunton police."

Kristy shook her head and closed her eyes. "I have never discussed any of it with Richard."

"Good. It would be embarrassing, what with this donation and all."

"I doubt he would have donated if he knew what you think of him."

Kristy, darling, you are one hundred per cent wrong. His knowing is the exact reason for his donation. With maybe even a couple cases of wine thrown in.

The better he played the part of thankful recipient, the safer Richard would feel. The less Richard knew, the more likely he was to be careless. Richard described Wallace as "sort of like an agent." A strange description for someone in the gambling profession. He'd give Moriarty a call tomorrow morning when he went out for the newspaper, out of Kristy's hearing. Moriarty would surely find Richard's description of Wallace interesting.

<h1 align="center">Sixteen</h1>

"Are you sure you haven't seen my book?" Mark called to Kristy. "Two weeks I'm looking for the damn thing. How could it disappear?"

Kristy answered from down the narrow hallway leading to the bathroom. "Don't come down here. What book?"

"The one I took to your mother's when you had the big argument. I haven't seen it since then."

"You must have left it there. I'll ask her if I ever talk to her again. What was it?"

"A mystery book. *The Three Coffins*. Very famous, and I wasn't even halfway through it."

"I'll buy you another one for your birthday. Are you ready?"

Mark, annoyed at not finding his book, called back. "Am I ready to be surprised, you mean?"

"Yes. And light the candle."

Kristy had been giggly all day, promising him a very special evening. He lit the candle and flicked off the light switch. The apartment grew romantically dim.

"Good," came Kristy's voice from the hallway. "Tell me when you're in bed."

He got back in bed wearing only his jeans. "I'm in bed. Let the show begin." Eying the hallway resulted in his expressing a simple reaction. "Wow!"

Kristy appeared all in white. White high heels. Sheer, white stockings held up by a white garter belt, the tiniest of white panties barely visible beneath a long, white lace vest held in place by a bow tied between her breasts.

Kristy pulled teasingly on one end of the bow ribbon until the vest spread open for a moment before fluttering gracefully closed. She pirouetted. The panties had no back to them.

"Now, some Shakespeare for your birthday, darling.

I'll be at charges for a looking-glass,
And entertain a score or two of tailors,
To study fashions to adorn my body:
Since I am crept in favour with myself,
I will maintain it with some little cost.
Shine out, fair sun, till I have bought a glass,
That I may see my shadow as I pass.

"I know I've given you a hard time lately over Richard and my brother. I didn't want to, but it's how I felt. It never seemed to be the time to talk about it, and I wasn't sure if you and I would weather the storm."

"You're sure now?"

"I'm sure. And instead of a *hard* time...you'd prefer something soft?" She opened her vest and let it flutter again.

"I think something soft would suit me fine. Where did you get that?"

"A store in the Village. Like it?"

Mark laughed. "No, take it back. Yes, it's beautiful. Come near and let me inspect it more closely."

"First, I have something for *you*." She flung a balled fist at Mark, and something landed on the bed next to him.

"A codpiece? An Elizabethan codpiece! Where the hell did you find this?"

"Same store. Put it on."

"Just this?"

"Just that. We'll dance together."

"There's no music."

"We'll make our own—as we always do."

He undressed and slipped the tiny piece of underwear on, feeling more than a little foolish.

Kristy laughed. "Mr. Macho Elizabethan." She walked over and put her arms around him. "I love you. I believe you want the best for me, no matter how I act. I want to give you an evening you'll never forget."

If the evening had ended then and there, he'd already experienced a ten-minute space of time he'd never forget. He was reasonably certain, however, the evening would continue—and it did. Memorably.

~ * ~

Mark groaned as the phone rang early the next morning. He and Kristy had been awake for half an hour. "At least they had the good manners to wait until we were finished," he groused.

"*Are* we finished?" Kristy's white ensemble lay scattered across the bottom of the bed.

"Finished! After last night and this morning, I'm a dead man."

"Poor baby. The phone."

Mark hopped from bed and picked up. "Hello." He faced Kristy and mouthed the words, "Your mother."

Kristy swung her legs over the edge of the bed and waited. She nodded to Mark's questioning look.

"Sure, she's here. Hold on." Kristy took the receiver, and Mark headed for the bathroom. When he returned, Kristy had already hung up.

"What did she want?" he asked.

"She wants to come to opening night. So does Richard."

"And you said?"

"What could I say? She's my mother. Two seats on the aisle, please."

Mark stepped back into his jeans. "How'd she sound?"

"Fine."

"Bring up any unpleasant topics?"

"Of course not."

"You'll be okay?"

"Yes. They'll be here tomorrow, so plan on seeing them tomorrow night, I'm guessing. She said she'd call between five and six."

Kristy got dressed. They were due at the theater in an hour. *Richard III* opened on Thursday, two days hence, and the troupe had its final run-through today. As they were about to go out the door, the phone rang again.

"I got it," said Mark. Kristy waited by the apartment door, her hand on the knob.

Mark hung up after a moment.

"Who was it?" asked Kristy.

Mark locked the door and said, "Moriarty. He wants to talk to me."

"Did I hear you tell him tonight?"

"Tonight's okay, isn't it? We'll be done early. We're eating at Phebe's, right? I told him to stop in."

"I guess. You want me to sit in?"

Mark took a breath. "I don't think so. The topic would not please you. You don't want to, do you?"

Kristy shook her head slowly. They continued their walk to the theater in silence.

The run-through of the play went smoothly, and Mark let Tony know it as they changed back into street clothes. "You're giving everyone extra energy, Tony. I think you've got Richard nailed. I almost regretted having to kill you."

"What are you doing tonight?" asked Tony.

"Hanging out at Phebe's with Kristy. You?"

"Home. I want to read through the play one more time. I'm off." Tony waved an insouciant farewell and left.

Mark left the other actors putting themselves back together and went upstairs to the tiny front office. When Moriarty had called earlier, he'd asked Mark whether he'd received the money Richard had promised. When Mark said he hadn't, Moriarty replied, "I didn't think so," but offered no more information. The topic would surely come up tonight—Mark looked at his watch—in an hour and a half when Moriarty promised to be in Phebe's.

He glanced at the phone as if staring would help him make up his mind. Finally, he tapped the appropriate buttons.

"May I speak with Wallace, please?" said Mark.

"Who is it?"

"My name is Mark Louis. I'm with the AWB Theatre Company."

"A *theater* company?"

A voice in the background said, "Give it here. Can I help you?"

"I'm looking for Wallace."

"Oh, Wallace. Wait a minute."

A moment later, "Yeah, this is Wallace."

"Wallace, this is Mark Louis from the theater company. I wanted to ask when your client planned to send us the donation you mentioned."

"The donation?"

"We haven't received it yet."

Wallace gave a disdainful snort. "Oh really?"

"Yes, really."

"I believe he may have changed his mind. Maybe he's decided to make a donation in another direction."

"Another direction? He never mentioned."

"He's a modest guy. Don't like to talk about his generosity."

"We're very disappointed."

Sarcasm smothered the reply. "Not as disappointed at his new beneficiary would be if the donation wasn't forthcoming."

"Well," Mark concluded, "I suppose there's nothing left to say then."

"How 'bout we try good-bye."

The phone went dead.

The ominous closing tone made Mark glad Moriarty was coming his way that evening.

~ * ~

Mark nursed a cold beer while he waited for Moriarty, already thirty minutes late. While he waited, he went over opening night, forty-eight hours away, tracking down any of the little things still needing attention. Barbara had done her part. Only eleven tickets remained to be sold, and he felt confident a full house would greet them when the curtain rose. Satisfied he'd met his theater obligations, he relished the opportunity to get back to the problem at hand, but he'd no more than begun to separate the different strands of the puzzle when Moriarty walked in the restaurant door.

"We gonna be alone?" Moriarty asked, pulling up a chair. "Freaking hot. A beer'll taste just fine, thank you."

"Yeah, Kristy had a drink with me and then went shopping to give us some time. She'll be here in an hour, give or take."

"I gotta pee. Get me a beer?"

"Sure."

When Moriarty returned to the table, a cold pint awaited him. After he took a long, satisfying pull on the drink, he said, "It's worth having the disease to get to the cure."

Mark laughed, and they touched glasses and drank again.

"What's the news?" said Mark.

"Your buddy's in trouble."

"My buddy? Richard?"

Moriarty drank again. "Yes, Richard. We had an opportunity to pull in a friend of Wallace's. Works for the same firm, so to speak. They're lowlifes. Real sewer dwellers. They know we can roust them any time, if we want to waste taxpayers' money and use a very expensive net to catch very tiny fish. The big ones are too smart, too...insulated." Mark cringed at his pronunciation. 'Inslalated.' "But we get some information from them now and then, and they're sometimes happy to give it to keep us out of their hair."

"So what did you learn?"

"You said you never got the money Richard promised you, right?"

"Yes, but I can tell you something about that."

"Let me tell you, first. You're not going to get it. Richard's in big time hot water with the wrong people—some racetrack bets gone wrong. He's repaying them enough to keep them happy, but he's got to make good soon."

"I see. I called Wallace today, and he said our 'benefactor' had chosen to put his money elsewhere. No wonder he said it with a laugh in his voice."

"Yeah, no wonder."

"How much money are we talking about?"

"My guy didn't know for sure. Maybe low six figures."

"Six figures! What half-a-million?"

"No, no, no. They wouldn't let it run up so high without a couple of broken legs involved. I said low six figures. I'm guessing a hundred... hundred fifty thousand tops. Ten percent a month would be ten, fifteen thousand, right?"

"Right."

"Something like that much is what Richard's gotta give them to keep himself..." Moriarty walked his fingers across the table. "Know what I mean?"

"I think I do. Didn't he have this debt when he promised us the money?"

"If he did, then he didn't get it." Moriarty tapped his temple. "Probably thought he had a sure thing somewhere and presumed this Wallace guy would send you some of the winnings. Didn't happen. He's in a serious spot."

"Richard's coming here tomorrow."

"Here, where?"

"He's coming to opening night along with Kristy's mother. Let me get you another beer." Mark signaled the waiter.

Moriarty drained his glass. "Thanks. I thought nobody was talking to nobody."

"Kristy's mother called and said she wanted to come. What could Kristy say?"

"Whose idea to bring Richard along?"

"Not Kristy's."

"He ain't driving her, is he?" Moriarty looked at Mark and lifted his eyebrows.

"They're driving. Of course, they're driving. Come on. He wouldn't...not on the way here. We know they're together."

"He gets money if she dies?"

"He gets access to a lot of money."

Moriarty shook his head. "Something screwy here."

"Damn true." The whole thing was playing out in a very odd manner. Betty changing her will to benefit Richard. Richard getting into mortal debt. Both of them attending opening night. "Screwy isn't the word. I can't figure. You want to tell me what's going on?"

"Like to, but I can't."

Mark leaned back as the waiter put two glasses of beer on the table. "Kristy's mom knows we're off tomorrow, so the four of us will probably have dinner together tomorrow night. They're arriving in the afternoon."

"Where they staying?"

"The Millenium down on Church Street."

Moriarty took a moment to wipe some foam from his upper lip. "Fancy place. Both of them stay there?"

"Yeah. They said they'd call us."

"So go to dinner and see what happens. Call me after."

"Where'll you be?"

"By the time you finish, home. Don't worry about waking me up. I ain't been sleeping too good."

"Heard from your wife?"

Moriarty's look told him he needed to talk about something else.

"I'll call when dinner's over," Mark promised.

"Mind if I keep you company till Kristy gets here?"

"Not at all. Maybe we'll get an insight."

"Insight, yeah. You get an insight; I'll get another beer. You?"

Mark laughed. "No, I'll wait for Kristy." The beer arrived quickly; the insight not at all.

Seventeen

"I very much wish this evening were over," said Mark as he and Kristy rode the elevator to the second floor of the Hotel Millenium. The small cocktail lounge where they'd met Richard the first time overflowed with well-dressed men and women, idling away their night in the Big Apple. Mark led Kristy through this noisy throng, past the bar to the quieter restaurant.

"I don't see them," said Mark.

"Sutor. Reservation for four," Kristy said to the host. "No, me either."

"They haven't arrived yet," the tuxedo-clad host explained with a gracious smile after checking his reservations book. "But I can show you to your table."

"Thanks, that'd be great," Mark replied. He and Kristy followed the host to a table next to a window. St. Paul's churchyard lay below.

"Nervous?" asked Mark. "About seeing Mom again, I mean."

"A little," said Kristy. "But I don't suppose anything sensitive will come up tonight."

"Is Richard paying for this...?"

"Here they come," said Kristy. Mark rose along with Kristy and put on his best smile.

"Mom." Kristy embraced her mother and kissed her cheek. The men shook hands, and everyone sat.

"I'm glad you could join us," said Betty.

"Don't be silly, Mom. We're glad you're coming to the opening."

"Your first opening night?' asked Mark.

"Yes," Betty answered, a hint of excitement in her voice. "My first peek at my actor daughter in New York. It's about time I learned what my baby is doing with her life."

"I've been spending it very happily, Mom." Mark felt Kristy's hand squeeze his thigh as she smiled at him.

The attention embarrassed Mark, but he returned Kristy's smile.

The waiter appeared with the wine list, which Richard accepted and perused. He hadn't said a word after hello, and as Betty studied her menu, Mark caught Kristy's eye and nodded questioningly at Richard. Kristy gave a tiny shrug.

The ordering ritual completed, Betty made a noise with her tongue and snapped her fingers, a quiet lady-like snap.

"Richard, I almost forgot. A man called for you today."

Richard came to attention. "Called? Here?"

"Yes. On the hotel phone when you were across the street. They rang my room by mistake. Both rooms are under Richard's name," Betty explained.

"What did he say?"

"I told him you'd be back shortly, but he didn't leave a message."

"A name? Did he leave a name?"

"I asked, but all he said was tell you he'd called, and you'd understand."

Richard's face froze for the briefest moment. He laughed. "Must've been Herb. He's been trying to sell me some Polish wine for months now."

"Polish wine?" said Mark.

"I've never tried any myself, but Herb's persistent. I ordered a more traditional wine tonight. I hope you like it." He directed this comment toward Kristy.

She acknowledged his attention, saying, "I'm sure it'll be fine."

Mark listened to mother and daughter converse through dinner, glad Kristy had guessed right. Touchy subjects stayed submerged, and the evening proceeded smartly. He tried a couple of times to talk to Richard, but Richard's mind was elsewhere.

After dinner, while awaiting coffee, the ladies excused themselves. Richard poured the final portion of the second bottle of wine into Mark's glass, filling it halfway.

"So, tomorrow's the big night, eh?" said Richard.

It was a lame opening line to pass the brief time the two of them would be alone, and Mark decided to raise the game.

"We haven't gotten the contribution you promised us, Richard. You have everyone's hopes real high at the company."

"You're kidding me! Here I am sitting wondering why you haven't thanked me." Mark enjoyed Richard's attempt to laugh things off. "You really haven't gotten it?"

Mark shook his head innocently.

"My associate should have sent the check by now. I thought he'd taken care of it. I'll get to him first thing tomorrow and see what the problem is."

Mark gestured dismissively, indicating he understood the oversight. "So, yes, tomorrow is a big night," he went on, explaining to Richard both the importance and harrowing nervousness of opening night. When the women returned, Mark excused himself, glad for a break and a moment alone. When he returned from the restroom, the coffee had been served and dessert had been rejected. The night ended soon after.

~ * ~

"So what did you and Richard discuss when Mom and I left you?" Kristy slipped into an AWB T-shirt and plopped onto the bed. Mark had come out of the bathroom hallway with a towel wrapped around his waist. He walked to the bed and stood in front of Kristy.

"I told him we didn't get his money yet."

"You didn't!"

"I did."

"How did he react?"

"Shocked. Amazed. He'll look into it pronto."

"Will he?"

"You haven't wanted me to tell you much about him. I know some things."

Kristy put her hand up. "Don't make him the evil hunchback again, please."

"Then I'll have to ask you not to ask."

"I won't."

Mark didn't want to leave a chasm of silence, so he said, "What did you and your mother talk about when you toddled off to pee?"

"'Toddled off to pee?' Seriously? And you're a Shakespearean actor?"

The brief laughter eased Mark's mood.

"What did you talk about?"

"I told her I still didn't agree with her, but I loved her. She said she didn't agree with me, but she loved me, too."

"The Age of Aquarius. Love conquers all."

"I suppose. I'm tired."

"Lucky for you, so am I."

"Lucky?"

Mark dramatically twirled the towel from around him. "I'd have swived you roundly, maiden."

Kristy gave a stage yawn. "With what?"

Mark looked down. "I'm tired, all right?"

"Tired? Try comatose."

"Jesus." He slunk into bed next to her. "I'll get even."

"I pray you will, milord."

They laughed, embraced, wrapped themselves around one another, and settled into sleep.

~ * ~

"I told you I'd get even," said Mark next morning. He got out of bed and dressed. Kristy lay under the sheet, smiling. "What should we have for breakfast?"

"Opening night morning? How about I go out and get a couple of decadent glazed donuts. We have orange juice in the refrigerator, and you can make the coffee."

"Do it. We've begun the day decadently. Let's keep it going."

Mark left and Kristy showered and dressed. She'd pulled her tank top over her as the phone rang. Mark opened the apartment door at the same moment.

Kristy picked up. "Hello? Oh, he just walked in the door. It's for you. Detective Moriarty." Mark took the phone, put the bag he carried on the table, and stepped toward the bathroom hallway.

"Hi, Detective. What's up?"

"They've given your friend one week to pay up."

"Wow!" Mark lowered his voice. "Or?"

"Ha! Or he won't like it."

"Does he have the money?"

"How do I know? He hasn't paid *yet*, so I doubt he does. Can you ask Kristy how easy it is to get, let's say, a hundred thousand dollars out of the company on short notice?"

Mark took a couple of steps more down the hallway. "I don't know if I can ask her or not. It's a subject we've steered clear of by mutual consent recently."

Moriarty slid into sarcasm. "You ain't got this 'mutual consent' thing with the mother, right? Ask her how quick Richard could get money outta the company if she dropped dead."

"That will be awkward."

"For Chrissake. It's the sixty-four dollar question, don't you think? Your lady friend's right there. Ask her. She'll forgive you."

Mark felt his soul plummet.

Moriarty said, "I know what you're thinking. She'll be mad at you. Forbidden topic blah, blah. Look, either you find out or maybe the next step is I arrest this guy after he murders your girlfriend's mother or arrest somebody else next week for murdering him. See how much your girlfriend likes you if you let that happen. Even more awkward, you think? Maybe worth her getting mad at you?"

"I see your point."

"What's your schedule today?"

"We're going to the theater around eleven."

"Listen, if you can't ask your lady friend, then you got to get away and talk to her mother. Ain't no two ways about it."

"Jesus, nothing's easy, is it? I'm glad I only have a small role tonight to worry about."

"You gotta a bigger role this afternoon. Star of the show."

"Or maybe I'll be seeing stars."

"You get back to me by six, the latest. If I don't hear from you, I'm coming by the theater."

"I'll look forward to you."

"The hell you will." Moriarty hung up.

Kristy poured coffee into Mark's cup. "What was that about?"

"You wouldn't be interested."

She shook her head. "Like two little boys. You bought four doughnuts."

"Opening night comes but once a year. Or whatever."

"Two for me?"

"Three if you want."

"Two will do, but I love you for your generosity."

Mark joined her at the table. "I hope you do."

Eighteen

Later in the afternoon, when Mark made a lame excuse to Kristy about his need to leave the theater for a while, she asked whether it had to do with Moriarty's morning call.

"You should be the detective," Mark responded with a resigned smile.

He'd called the Millenium earlier and found Betty in her room. She agreed to meet him in the hotel bar at three o'clock, and he'd specified they meet without Richard.

Betty, dressed in a short, white dress with a pale pink and blue print of small flowers, didn't rise from the small round table when Mark arrived. Her dress rode nicely up her thighs, and Mark scolded himself again for noticing. He chose a spot across from her where he couldn't see her legs.

"Drink?" she said. She had a glass in front of her.

"No, I can't. I have to be on my best behavior."

"Opening night?"

"Exactly."

"Me, too. A spritzer," she said, explaining the glass in her hand. "What did you want to see me about? As if I didn't know."

Her 'As if I didn't know' broke the ice of the moment, but Mark knew the plunge into the water would be frigid. The waiter's appearance briefly postponed the ordeal.

"Just a diet cola."

"I'm fine," Betty responded to the waiter's glance.

"Richard is in debt," Mark began.

"I know."

"You know?"

"He asked me whether he could borrow one hundred fifty thousand dollars from either me or the company."

Mark exhaled audibly. "Bold move on his part."

"Bold but useless. I said no. I won't go into the conversation, but, in short, the company pays him handsomely, and he has to live on that."

"Did he say why he needed the money?"

"Personal reasons, he said."

"Want to know the real reason?"

Betty motioned with her left hand, inviting him to go on. She sipped her drink.

Mark allowed the waiter to put his soda down on the table and walk away. "He owes a lot of money to gamblers here in New York. You must know he's a big gambler. He got in with the wrong crowd, an unforgiving crowd, and he's in trouble. They want their money."

"'In with the wrong crowd.' You make him sound like a teenager."

Mark held her gaze. "These are not teenagers he's dealing with, nor does he have a teenage problem. Can I ask you a question?"

"What else have you ever done?"

"Yeah, well. What right does Richard have to company money if you're gone?"

Betty sat back in her chair. "What an abrupt young man you are. If I disappear from the face of the earth, Richard is entitled to sign checks from the company on his own for a period of thirty days until a second signatory is assigned. Answer your question?"

"You're flaunting opportunity in his face."

"Opportunity? Opportunity? Yes, the opportunity to finally close your mouth for good, Mark. Let me be blunt, as blunt as you have chosen to be. There is nothing wrong with Richard. He is a fine young man. He married my daughter to my great delight. Kristy became disenchanted with him, ultimately, perhaps due to meeting you. I know Richard is a fine man. I will do anything I need to do to prove it, if only to you. I know you have some track record in dealing with things of...I was going to say of this nature, but your record is in ferreting out murderers. There is nothing for you to ferret out here. I don't know what Kristy sees in you. I see very little. If she wants to toss her life away on...on you, the theater, this city..." She paused to calm herself. "...there's nothing I can do about it. But I am as certain of Richard's loyalty, his affection for my family, as I've ever been of anything in my life, and I'm certain he'll be able to work out any problems he has. Do I make myself clear?"

Profound mortification swept over Mark. "I'd have to say you do." He fought hard to keep eye contact with Betty. Responding to her tirade by dropping his gaze like a scolded child would only deepen his mortification. He rose from the table. "And I hope you don't live...or die...to regret it."

She puffed her lips dismissively, raised her glass, and nodded with finality. Mark left the table.

~ * ~

"So how did you enjoy your afternoon?" Kristy asked.

The actors had begun to get into costume for the opening. Shows usually began at eight, but openings were advanced an hour so the cast could have its opening night party at a reasonable time. Conversation in the dressing rooms flagged as butterflies crowded the airspace.

Mark had walked back uptown after his meeting with Betty, stopping to phone Moriarty on the way. Moriarty hadn't picked up.

"I didn't enjoy it. This whole awful episode is getting on my nerves. I wish it had never happened. I wish it were over."

"Ssshh. Calm down. Emotional, aren't we?"

"If you see Moriarty in the theater, tell me."

"You bet, Sherlock."

Mark turned on her.

"Look, I don't know what the hell you think I'm doing. *I* think I'm trying to help you *and* your mother, but she's either so goddamned stubborn or so goddamned stupid that when something happens, it's going to be her own goddamned fault, and maybe yours, too."

Angrier than he could ever remember being at Kristy, he spun away and buried himself in the gentlemen's dressing room. He had to talk with Moriarty, the only person other than himself, who feared the future.

When Mark calmed down, he went up to the front office to try Moriarty again, but before Moriarty's phone even rang, someone began banging on the front door of the theater. He looked out the small office window, and there stood Moriarty. After tossing his phone on the desk, he stepped outside the building and closed the door behind him.

"We going somewhere?" asked Moriarty.

"No. You're late. I've been calling you."

"Cell finally died. Been meaning to get a newer one. You want to talk here on the steps?"

"It's private enough."

"Okay. So what happened today?"

"Betty adamantly insists Richard is on the up and up. She told me off good, but she did say he'd asked her for money—a hundred and fifty thousand—and he'll have complete authority to sign the company checks if she is out of the picture."

"She told you this?"

"She did."

Moriarty leaned back against the railing. "You tell her he needed the money for gambling debts?"

"I did. She sloughed it off."

"Nice. So here's what we got. Richard is one step away from broken legs, or worse, unless he gets a hundred fifty thousand bucks—your figure. Your friend's mother has it and won't part with it, but if she's removed from the game board, he can pay off his debts and maybe live happily ever after. How's it sound to you?"

Mark flung an arm up. "Sounds terrible to me. I know...*we* know Betty is in Richard's way, and they'll be spending tonight and the next day or two together. Plus there's the drive back to Brunton and the days that follow."

"So you think he plans to get rid of her?"

"How do I know? Why not? He's done it before."

"Says you."

"Says me."

"So how, you think?"

"Everything's been with a car so far. The father, probably. The brother, for certain. I think he might stage a car accident on the way back to Brunton."

"I can take the day off and follow him in my car," said Moriarty.

"If they leave for home early enough tomorrow, and I have enough time to get back for the performance, I'll go with you. I'll ask about it tonight."

"You more worried about Shakespeare than your girlfriend's mother?"

Mark snapped, "I've warned them. Both of them. Betty in particular. I have no way of making excuses for not showing up at the theater. If I can go with you, I will. If I can't, I'll leave it to you."

"A bit touchy, ain't you?"

"You try convincing people who refuse to be convinced."

"No thanks. Can I stay for the play?"

Mark took a deep breath. "Of course. Come in. I'll see what Barbara has left."

~ * ~

At seven-ten, the play underway, Mark peeked into the audience from offstage. He found Betty and Richard in their seats as Tony Babbitte, dressed somberly as Richard Third, waited for his regal soon-to-be predecessor to exit the stage. Tony spoke to the audience, revealing ugly thoughts.

Now is the winter of our discontent
Made glorious summer by this sun of York
And the clouds that did lour on our house
Are in the deep bosom of the ocean buried.

Betty smiled and whispered something to Richard. How could her confidence in Richard be so high she could sit with him and benignly smile after everything he'd told her? Mark didn't appear on stage for a considerable time yet, so he went back downstairs and watched with satisfaction and a great deal of relief as the play swirled around him.

Nineteen

Mark grasped Tony's hand and pumped it as the cast and invited guests milled about the downstairs lobby. "Tony, you know it. You know it, don't you?" The play had been well-performed and well-received.

Tony beamed. "It *was* good, wasn't it?"

"We're going to lose you because of this role. I know we are. Just like we lost Don." Don Lovett was a former company member who had moved on to movies.

Tony threw his head back and laughed as someone else touched his arm for attention.

"Wait until we get to Phebe's to congratulate him," Mark advised Kristy as she tried to take her turn with Tony. "People are all over him here."

"I'm glad your mood's improved,"

"Forget it," said Mark. "Opening night and all."

"Here come my mom and Richard."

"Richard and all."

"Shh. Did you both enjoy the play?"

"It was wonderful," said Betty, "but you said you celebrate tonight. Where? Not down here, I hope."

"No, no. Across the street. You've heard me mention Phebe's."

"Indeed I have, and I get to see it tonight?"

"Absolutely."

Betty touched Kristy's arm. "We're going home tomorrow. You and Mark will come downtown for a final drink tonight, won't you, after your party?"

"At your hotel?" said Mark.

"Yes."

Mark tried to discourage the idea. "The party may last a while for us. Managing director, you know, so I really should stay. You sure you want to be up so late? You'll probably be leaving early tomorrow."

"Hotel check-out's not till eleven. Besides, late's no problem on a night like this. I'm looking forward to my first opening night theater party," said Betty. She touched Kristy's arm again. "Across the street, you say?"

"Yes, across the street and two blocks north. Out the door and left to you."

"We'll find our way and meet you there. Tell them you enjoyed the play, Richard."

"Oh, I did. Of course, I did. Memorable, really."

"He's been absent all day," said Betty, tapping her temple. "Business calls. He always seems to miss the one he most wants to get. Another call today from the Polish wine merchant, and he missed it."

Kristy hugged her mother and stepped back. "Mark and I have to get changed. We'll be there as soon as we can. Wait, stay here." She ran in and out of the ladies' dressing room. "Show these at the door. Only invited guests in the private room at Phebe's tonight."

Betty took the tickets. "How exclusive. Thanks. See you there."

After Betty and Richard left, Mark said, "Your mother seems in an exceptionally good mood tonight."

"Makes up for Richard's rotten mood."

"What a pair. Go change. I'll wait right here for you."

"I'll be quick."

~ * ~

Richard sat in the front seat of the cab as Mark, Kristy, and Betty talked in the back. It was nearly midnight.

"So many happy, excited people," said Betty. "Lovely to see, Kristy, darling. I really had no idea how exciting one of these evenings could be."

"Ah, but now we have to go back and do it night after night, Betty," Mark explained. "With no parties afterward. It's work, but if you enjoy it, as Kristy does, there's nothing else you'd ever want to do. Wasn't your daughter terrific tonight?"

"I wanted to get up and smack her when she spit in that poor young man's face."

"That poor young man killed my father and husband! He had it coming."

"But you married him anyway?"

Mark bit his tongue and refrained from commenting. He let mother and daughter banter, surprised they could be ignorant of the irony so obvious to him. When the cab pulled up in front of the Millenium, Richard paid the driver, and they entered the hotel.

This time, they rode the escalator to the restaurant floor, Betty leading the way. Over her shoulder she said, "Richard, get us a table at the bar. Then you can go up and check your messages. Heaven forbid you missed another one."

"I will. Why he doesn't call my cell number, I can't imagine, but I hope there is a message. I'd like to take a chance on the Polish wine before he gives it to someone else. It's different."

Richard procured a table, and Betty, Kristy, and Mark seated themselves.

"Sit a moment, Richard," Betty said, smiling. "Let's order first. Then I'll go up with you. These shoes have been killing me all night. I'm thinking of suing Bloomingdale's."

After the waiter took their order, Richard and Betty rose from the table. Richard said, "We'll be back before he brings the drinks. They're so damned slow in here."

Betty stroked her daughter's cheek. "I'll be right back, sweetheart."

Mark and Kristy watched Betty and Richard turn the corner to the elevators.

Mark put his hand atop Kristy's. "I think this trip did your mother a world of good. I mean regarding how she thinks of you and how you spend your time."

"God, I hope so. She does seem to be impressed with us." Kristy laughed and squeezed Mark's hand. "I love you, Mark. In all of this swirl about Richard, my mother, opening night, and everything, I want you to know. The world will calm down soon. Our happy routine will return."

"Yes, I hope it will. I love you, too, darling. Very, very much."

The drinks arrived quicker than anticipated, and Mark and Kristy sipped theirs and enjoyed their still radiant opening night glow.

"Here comes my mom," said Kristy.

Betty came around the corner from the elevators, paused, and glanced back. She said something, smiled, and waved. When she reached the table, she indicated surprise at the quick arrival of their drinks.

"Richard's going to end up with ice water instead of Scotch on the rocks." She sat and took the first sip of her white wine.

"Where is he?" said Mark. "Did he get any messages?"

"I guess so. He said he was going down to the lobby to meet the Polish wine merchant."

"Right now?" said Kristy.

Betty nodded, taking another sip of wine. "Kristy, I want to tell you again I had no idea how exciting what you were doing could be. If I were thirty years younger, I might go in for it myself. How many roles does Shakespeare provide for fifty-year-old women?"

"I'm sure we could find one if you wanted to give it a try," said Mark. Lady Macbeth rose in his mind.

"But tell me more about where the play goes from here. What do you do now the play is a success?"

Mark laughed. "It hasn't exactly been proven successful yet. Parents of cast members are not generally the most respected of literary critics. No offense."

Mark went on to explain the company's hopes for some reviews to drum up interest and moved on to what transpired in the day-to-day life of the theater.

The waiter appeared, and they ordered another three-drink round. Richard's drink sat, the ice dwindling to mere dots in the glass.

Anxiety gnawed at Mark as they talked on. When he emptied his second drink, he said, "It's been too long."

"Too long?" said Betty.

"Richard shouldn't be this long, even if he met whoever. He knows we're here."

"Mmm, I think you're right," said Betty. "We're finished, and it's very late. Let's go rouse him. We should at least get to say good-bye to one another."

Without Richard to pay the bill, Mark put eighty dollars on the table.

Kristy smiled at him. "Don't you want your change?"

"I love you most when you're most sarcastic. The one thing I like about Richard—he always picks up the check."

Betty preceded them down the escalator to the hotel lobby.

"I don't see him. Do you?" asked Betty.

"No," said Mark. "No."

"Me either. I'll call his cell," said Kristy. Mark waited. "He isn't picking up."

"Maybe he's in his room," said Mark.

"We can try," said Betty.

"Why wouldn't he pick up?" asked Kristy.

Mark led them to the elevators. "What floor?" he asked.

"Seven," said Betty.

Mark hit the button, and they rode up in silence.

"This way," said Betty.

She turned right out of the elevator and went to the end of the hall. "That's me, and that's Richard," she said, indicating the final two rooms in the corridor.

She knocked at the end door but got no answer. Mark stepped up and knocked louder. "I don't like this," he said.

"Don't like what?" said Kristy.

"He should answer," said Mark.

"Maybe he and the wine fellow went somewhere to have a drink," said Kristy.

"He wouldn't leave the hotel without telling us, business or not," Mark said. He knocked more insistently. Nothing happened.

"Try again," said Betty.

Mark banged the door hard.

"Do you have a key to this room?" asked Mark.

"No," said Betty. "The rooms connect inside, but the doors, I know, are locked."

"Let's try knocking on the connecting door anyway," said Mark.

Betty took out her key card and slid it into the slot above her door handle. The green light appeared, and they entered. Mark went straight to the connecting door. He opened the door on Betty's side and tried the second door. No luck. He banged on it hard.

"Damn."

"He must have gone out," said Kristy, perplexed at Mark's insistence. "What's the big deal?"

"Kristy, darling, listen. Richard is in debt, and do you know who he's in debt to?" Mark didn't wait for an answer. "These are gambling debts to the wrong people. Gambling debts up to here." Mark drew his hand across his neck. "He can't pay them, and he has no time left to pay them. He's overdue. These people he's in debt to don't like to be kept waiting, if you know what I mean."

"He doesn't gamble much," said Kristy in a weak rebuttal.

"He does, Kristy. Betty, do you think you could have the hotel open up his room?"

"I...I could ask," she said.

"You're worried, Mom?" said Kristy.

"Richard asked me for the loan of a hundred fifty thousand dollars, sweetheart."

"What!" Kristy cried. "For what?"

"He wouldn't tell me."

"You both are scaring me," Kristy said.

"It's about time," Mark snapped.

Kristy's eyes flashed anger, but she didn't respond.

"Let me call the desk," said Betty. It took a while, but finally someone arrived at the room authorized to do what she wanted.

"You'll have to sign this, please," said an overweight, baby-faced older man in a self-important monotone.

Betty signed the paper, and the man, Mr. Frother by name, led them into the hallway and opened the door of Richard's room.

Mark walked in first. The manner in which he said, "Oh, shit," halted those behind him. Kristy, however, couldn't contain her curiosity. She pressed forward next to Mark.

"Oh my God! Mark!" She and Mark faced each other then looked back at the bed. Richard lay sprawled across it, face down, a small but obviously effective wound visible in the back of his head.

Twenty

Detective Moriarty sat in Mark's apartment at the dining table drinking coffee the next afternoon.

He grimaced and set the cup down. "Whew! This is crap coffee."

Mark took a seat across from the detective. "Look, I'm drinking it, aren't I?"

"It's still crap. No offense."

"I don't make coffee very often," Mark explained.

"Never again would be too soon. Where's Kristy?"

"With her mother."

"She can do better than this, I hope."

"She can. She does. So, what do you know?"

Moriarty looked at his watch. "What time you gotta go to the theater?"

"Six normally, but I could walk in at nine-thirty and still have time to get into costume. It's four o'clock. You have five hours of information?"

"No. Got five minutes maybe. Not my case, you understand. I'm in on it as a courtesy."

Mark gestured Moriarty to begin.

"We can't find anybody who saw Richard after he left you people."

"Betty saw him heading down into the lobby."

"Right, besides her, but she didn't see him actually reach the lobby. Cameras didn't pick him up, but there are blind spots. The people who work in the lobby don't remember seeing him."

"Would you expect them to remember everybody who passes through the lobby?"

"No, of course not. But the fact remains. We don't know who he met in the lobby, or if he met anyone, or even if he made it to the lobby."

"Why'd he even get off the elevator if he was continuing to the lobby?"

"Your lady friend's mother said they rode the one elevator that don't go to the lobby. It's, and I quote, 'for the convenience of the restaurant patrons.' Separates the riff from the raff, I guess. He had to get off it and take the escalator the rest of the way."

"You want orange juice instead of this?"

Moriarty waved off the offer.

Mark pushed his own cup away. "So, you think maybe the guy called him from the lobby and invited him to come down? Or may he went up? Betty said someone was looking for him yesterday and today. Or maybe Richard forgot something and went back up to his room and never got to the lobby? Or they met and went back to his room together?"

"All possibilities, my friend. There was nothing on his cell phone to help out."

"This was the gambling debt, no doubt?"

"You can suggest something else?"

"Polish wine wars?"

"Yeah, right," Moriarty scoffed.

"Did you talk to the people he actually owed the money to?"

"*Omerta.* You heard of it?"

"I've seen movies. Code of silence."

"The rat who mentioned the debt to me won't go any further. Not about a murder, a contract hit. Guaranteed. Hell, he probably don't know anything, anyway."

"Find the gun?"

"No gun, and whoever did it is already back in Hoboken."

"They bring people in from Hoboken?"

"How the hell you solve mysteries? Not Hoboken. Anywhere. I'm making an example."

"Oh." Mark tried his homemade coffee again but put the cup down with a clank. "Got your gun? Shoot me if I lift this to my mouth again."

"I'm thinking of shooting you for giving it to me in the first place."

Mark took the two cups and dumped the coffee into the sink.

"You're going to hear from the sewer alligators they get a taste of that stuff," said Moriarty.

"Never mind. What happens now?"

"We talk to people, look for the gun. Never find it, not if this is a professional job, which it looks like it is."

"So he's dead and it's over?"

Moriarty shrugged. "Happens. The lesson is, choose your friends more carefully. Kristy okay?"

"I think so. She and her mom commiserated. We took her mother over to Kristy's apartment last night. She didn't want to stay in the hotel. I came back here."

"Kristy stay with her?"

"Yeah. One of Kristy's roommates was away, and she imposed on the other two to give her mother her own room for last night and tonight. Kristy stayed on the sofa. I think she's sleeping there tonight again, but I'm not sure. Kristy'll drive her back home tomorrow morning."

"Kristy make the show tonight?"

"The show must go on."

Moriarty rose. "I'll keep you up on things if there's anything worth keeping up on."

"Thanks, and if I can do anything to help, you'll let me know."

"There is one thing."

"What?"

"Learn to make coffee."

"Right."

~ * ~

"What time are you meeting your mother?" Mark asked Kristy the following morning, a Saturday. The second performance of the play had been successfully enacted. Barbara's invitations plus good word-of-mouth had reached three neighborhood newspapers. They'd sent representatives to see the play, and the actors looked forward to the reviews. Kristie's mother insisted she did not need coddling and wanted some time alone besides, so Kristie spent Friday night with Mark on Avenue B.

Kristy paced the apartment. "I told her I had to be at the theater by seven, so we counted backwards, and we figured eleven o'clock would give us plenty of sleep and me plenty of time to make the round trip to Brunton."

"I'll go with you if you want."

Kristy walked around the dining table to where Mark glanced out the window and put her arms around him. "Oh, Mark." She hugged him silently.

Mark expected to see teary eyes when he next looked at Kristy, but, no, her eyes gleamed, instead, with trust.

"I'm impressed with the way you're holding up."

She closed with him again and tucked her head next to his. "I want you to know I'm giving up my apartment share in Chelsea." She stepped back.

"When did you decide that?"

"There's a second part."

"Which is?"

"Please let me do this. I want to live with you but not here. This place is a wreck."

Mark laughed.

"What's funny?"

"Your face. Go on."

"I want to get us a better apartment."

"You mean I'll be a kept man?"

"Yes."

"I like it."

"You do?"

"Sure. This place is a wreck."

Kristy giggled and hugged him.

"I have to get my mother in..." She looked at the bedside clock. "...seventy-five minutes. Lie down and hold me."

They settled into bed and for nearly an hour Mark did as asked. He simply held Kristy, and for a short while she even napped.

~ * ~

"Want me to go up and get her?" Mark asked when they double-parked in front of Kristy's Twentieth Street apartment building. The street was lined with beautiful brownstone buildings like Kristy's, once individual homes for the well-to-do, now chopped into apartments.

"Okay. You go. I'll watch the car."

"I'll try to speed her along."

Mark went up the steps of Kristy's brownstone. He pressed the buzzer and waited for the responding buzz from the front door. He entered and climbed the stairs to the third floor. Betty opened the door.

"Mark, hello. I didn't expect you. Are you making the trip with us?"

"Hi, Betty. Yes, I figured it might be better for Kristy. Give her some company on the ride back. How are you? Anybody here?"

Mark looked over the large, well-furnished apartment and had a sudden desire for the new apartment Kristy had in mind.

"No, everyone's out. I'm managing. It was quite a shock, as you can imagine."

"He fell in with the wrong crowd and had the wrong bad habit."

"And you tried to warn us."

"I doubt whether it would have made much difference. When the bad guys want their money, they want their money."

"Let's not talk about it."

"Sure. Where's your luggage?"

"In there." She indicated one of the two bedrooms. "Let me freshen up. Richard's bag is with mine. I threw his stuff into it."

"I'll get both bags."

Betty left for the bathroom, and Mark went into the bedroom. He'd spent a night there once when Kristy's roommates were off somewhere. Looking it over, he felt another surge of dissatisfaction with his own grungy apartment. His ego could abide Kristy's providing a new home for them. It would be her apartment, and he would have moved in with her, no different from her having moved in with him. Happened all the time, didn't it?

Two large suitcases, one black, the other green and brown plaid, stood on the floor. He noticed part of a garment sticking out the side of the black suitcase, Richard's, no doubt. It gave him an excuse to open the suitcase, and Mark wondered whether Betty or even the police had gone through it. He heard water running in the bathroom and seized the opportunity.

He pushed the green and brown plaid suitcase aside and snapped open the fasteners of the black suitcase. He lifted the top and saw an array of shirts, but only as an aside. A piece of what looked like pink or light orange rubber protruded from under the clothing. Mark's stomach plummeted. He threw back the top of the suitcase, dug under the clothing, and pulled out an over-the-head mask of George W. Bush. He stared dumbly at the mask when a noise from behind made him drop it.

Betty stood in the doorway. Mark retrieved the mask and held it up.

"In Richard's suitcase. I told you. My God. This is proof. At least for us. But how did the police miss...?" He returned his glance to the open suitcase. The spine of a book caught his eye. John Dickson Carr— *The Three Coffins*. He dropped the mask and picked up the book.

"My book. How the hell did Richard get my book? I left this at your house the day you and Kristy had the argument."

Mark stared into the suitcase. He pulled a white garment out—a bra. A women's blouse. Panties and a small pink hairbrush. He spun and gaped at Betty.

"Whose suitcase...this isn't..."

"It's my suitcase, Mark."

His eyes still on Betty, Mark put the mask down, perplexed.

"*You* were the one? You *couldn't* have been the one." Mark racked his memory. Where was Betty when her husband was killed? He didn't know. When Kristy was almost hit? When Brian was killed? He couldn't remember. Betty? Impossible! But the suitcase...No wonder she never believed anything he told her about Richard.

"My God," said Mark. "You..." The doorbell rang.

"It's probably Kristy," said Betty. "Close the suitcase." She walked across the living room.

Kristy's voice reached the bedroom. "I found a parking spot, so I came up to help."

Mark shoved everything back into the suitcase and slammed it shut. He rose and walked into the living room on weak knees.

"I found a spot," Kristy repeated. "What do you need help with?"

"There are two suitcases," said Betty. "Mark, will you get them?"

Mark reentered the bedroom. Where the hell had he gone so wrong? Betty murdering off her family? Richard merely a gambler whose luck had run out, and who had nothing to do with any of this? It didn't seem possible. It *wasn't* possible.

Kristy called to him. "Come on, Mark. What's keeping you?"

Mark lifted the two suitcases and carried them to the living room.

"I'm glad Mark's coming along with us," said Betty.

Kristy smiled at Mark and said, "I wasn't looking forward to driving home alone."

"Anything for you, sweetie," said Mark, now gladder than ever he'd promised to make the trip with Kristy. He'd get the whole story out of Betty today. Hell, he would *not* go home without it. "I'm ready if both of you are. Shall we go?" Mark led the way, and the two women followed him out of the apartment.

Down on the street, Mark waited while Kristy opened the trunk. He tossed the suitcases inside and slammed the trunk lid down.

"Want to drive?" Kristy asked Mark.

"No. You and your mom can sit up front. I'll be more comfortable in back."

Everyone climbed in, Kristy started the engine, and the trip got underway.

Twenty-one

"Did Richard have any family?" Mark asked. He and Betty were alone in the living room. Kristy had left to visit the funeral director to make arrangements for Richard. Betty had seen to it she and Mark stayed behind by insisting to her daughter she wanted to have a private conversation with Mark.

"Maybe she's going to give you her blessing at long last," Kristy said as she got into the family BMW. "You deserve it."

"We'll see," Mark responded as Kristy drove off.

"Want a drink?" Betty asked. "I'm having one."

Mark shook his head. He sat on the sofa, bracing himself for Betty's explanation.

Betty poured herself a healthy Scotch and sat in a chair across from Mark. "He was an only child whose parents died a few years ago. There's an uncle in Texas and a few cousins scattered around, but it's fallen to us to arrange the funeral. Kristy did speak to his uncle from your apartment."

"Yes, I know."

"Are you certain you don't want one?" She indicated her drink. "You may need one soon."

"I can't."

"The show again?"

"Driving. The show."

Betty was slow to start, so Mark initiated the conversation. "Did you murder…"

She held up her hand. "I did, but I want to show you something." She put her glass on the coffee table and returned to the bar. She went behind the bar and bent down. When she stood, she held a business card between her fingers.

"What is it?" Mark tried to compartmentalize Betty's stunning admission, so he could pay attention to whatever else she had to say.

Betty gave Mark the card.

The card read, *Gordon's Novelties. 929 Broadway, New York City.*

"Did you read it?" asked Betty. "Let me have it." She walked back to the bar and lifted a pack of matches from the bar top. Mark noted the bright red matchbook cover. She tore one match from the pack, lit it, and held it to the business card. Betty laid the blackening paper in a glass ashtray, and when the flame died, she returned to her chair. She took her Scotch from the tabletop and sipped.

"What am I supposed to make of that?" asked Mark.

"It's where the mask came from."

"And from the beginning, you let me tell you Richard was the one. What a chump I must have seemed." Mark fastened his gaze on Betty. "Can you tell me why you set out to murder your own family?"

Betty was about to sip her drink again, but registering Mark's sentence, she lowered the glass. "Murder my family? What on earth are you talking about?"

"You have the mask. You just now admitted you murdered your husband and son."

"Mark, I did no such thing. I *said* no such thing. How can you even think…? I shot *Richard* in his hotel room. I killed him because *he* murdered my son, tried to murder my daughter, and almost certainly murdered my husband."

Mark's head spun. "You...I...I must be losing my mind. You murdered Richard because *Richard* was after your family?"

"Why are you acting so surprised? You accused him to me. You were certain about Richard from the very beginning. You tried to move mountains, hell, and high water to get me to believe you. Now, you act astonished when I say you were right?"

"I can't believe this," said Mark. "But you had the mask. You said..."

"I can't believe *you*. If there was anyone I hoped I could talk to and explain and would understand what I did and why I did it, it was you."

Mark held up his hands. "Let's do this slowly. Start at the beginning."

"*You* were the beginning. I didn't want you to know then, but I can tell you now. I *have* to tell you now. I believed what you told me almost from the moment you began telling it to me."

"About Richard and the death of your son?"

Betty looked down. "Yes."

"You could have fooled me."

Her head snapped up. "I *intended* to fool you. Richard was... was...an absolutist, for lack of a better word. Whatever he wanted, he wanted to the exclusion of all else. Obsessive might be the more appropriate word. Through high school, college, his early years with us, his pursuit of Kristy—I saw this quality as a *strength*, a quality other people who knew him saw as dedication."

She said "dedication" as if it were a synonym for "excrement."

"When put to a positive purpose, it can be admirable, don't you see? Now, you come along and accuse him of acting in a manner I recognize as part of his personality, but to a purpose impossible to fathom." She said the final three words slowly. "I recognized the behavior you described but couldn't process the goal. Understand?"

Mark nodded once.

"I admire how you thought I deserved to know what you knew. I wanted you to continue to tell me what you found out, but I didn't want to join up with your…investigation, because if Richard did what you claimed he did, I wanted the ability to act with independence."

Mark's stomach ached from tension. He wished he'd taken the drink Betty had offered. Kristy could have driven home, and he didn't go on stage until almost ten o'clock. Too late now. He couldn't interrupt this. He watched jealously as Betty took a long sip from her glass.

"I decided to see on my own what I could find out. I looked through Richard's desk the first chance I got and found the card I showed you. I called Gordon's and asked whether I could purchase a mask of President Bush there."

Betty paused and took another sip of her drink. The glass neared empty. "I could buy one, but I had no real hope of having the store remember Richard buying the mask. I did think to ask whether they did mail order, but they don't, so there would be no record of its being shipped to Richard. So I simplified it. Either Richard still had the mask, or he didn't. I looked over his office and didn't find it. One day at the warehouse, I made an excuse to borrow his car. I knew he kept his apartment key on the same ring with his car key. I found the mask hidden in his apartment. *Hidden*," she finished softly. "I don't believe he ever knew Kristy told you or *anyone* about the face of the driver who almost hit her, and he wouldn't have had access to the police report and Brian's description of the driver."

"No," said Mark. "Only I had that."

"He had no reason to believe the mask was in any way dangerous to him, so he kept it and hid it."

"Maybe he planned to use it again. Where did you find it?"

"Way up on the back of a shelf in his bedroom closet." She took a breath, looked to the ceiling, uncrossed and recrossed her legs, left leg on top. "That was really all I needed. After that, it came at me in a whirlwind. He needed money. I knew about his gambling. I found a great deal of evidence of it when I went through his things. When the police finally go through his things, they'll find the same information. I had him on my mind constantly. There was my husband's death. In a car, as you know. Easily accomplished, I think, if Richard put his mind to it. He could have met my husband in the rest area, as you imagined. Did you know there's a lover's lane off the rest area?"

"Kristy mentioned it."

"He could have hidden himself, his car, there and seen to it my husband...had his accident. Kristy. Then Brian."

Betty stopped to compose herself.

"And you decided to settle things yourself," said Mark.

"You're damned right I did. I don't know whether I would have been able to if you hadn't left your book behind the day Kristy and I argued. I owe you a great debt."

"My book? What do you mean?" Mark asked softly.

"Well, you may have guessed by now I instigated the argument with my daughter. I wanted the two of you, especially Kristy, to have a great distance from me while I did what I knew I had to do—give Richard the opportunity to...well, you know what I mean...prove himself. The scene with Kristy was very painful." She paused a moment. "Your book helped immensely. How would I satisfy myself against Richard? Your book told me how—chapter seventeen, method number five."

"I didn't get that far," said Mark. "What does chapter seventeen, method number five suggest?"

"Illusion. It suggests illusion. *After* the victim is murdered, make others think he's still alive. Your Mr. Carr suggests dressing as the victim and appearing in public. I couldn't very well do that, but I could say goodbye to him in front of the elevators in full view of you and Kristy when he was already lying dead in his room."

Mark's understanding of what she'd done opened like a springtime flower. "When the trouble with his debt arose, you manufactured the person looking for him, didn't you? No one called him when you were with us in New York. Richard's Polish wine merchant was merely Richard's explanation for the calls you made him believe he got."

"Yes, I manufactured Richard's pursuer. *I* was the only pursuer he had. I made certain both of our hotel rooms were in his name, so he'd believe I was getting calls meant for him."

"He *was* under pressure to pay off the debt—real pressure. The police detective I know told me."

Betty looked down at her empty glass. "His insistence about the loan he wanted told me that, too. When he realized my answer was final, I knew what he had to do, and I knew what I had to do. I had to give him every incentive to act against me, so I changed the will. I wanted him to realize there was an out for him, a way he could write whatever checks he needed and be off the hook. And I watched him."

"Do you...did he give any indication he planned to harm you?"

Betty spread her hands. "His eyes. How he looked at me. I could see it in his eyes. I cringed whenever he suggested something involving the car. But now, thank goodness, he'll have no chance. But I wasn't trying to protect myself, understand. I wanted to settle up with him for the past." She stood and went to the bar to pour another drink.

Mark waited for her to sit again. "He would've had to be very clever if he went after you. He knew I suspected him. Did you ever mention to him you called Rogers, the lawyer from Haverford?"

"I mentioned Rogers to him, and that I'd checked on the time of the meeting. Richard must have assumed I'd called him. I didn't specifically say so."

"So you must have asked Richard about the hour's discrepancy in the meeting times, too."

"After I checked with Rogers about it on my own and saw what my husband had written in his appointment book, I asked Richard if the meeting had been moved up an hour. He said no, of course."

"Richard connected your mentioning Rogers and your question about the time of the meeting. He had to."

"I knew enough not to mention where I'd gotten my information. I kept you out of it."

"Didn't matter. Richard found out I was checking on him when you spooked him into calling the lawyer. When I called Rogers the second time, he told me he mentioned to Richard my asking about the change in time. Richard hoped making a big contribution to the theater would somehow end my interest in him. He wanted to buy me off or at least play on any uncertainties I had and on my regard for your family."

"But you had no uncertainty."

"No, I didn't. Not until this afternoon for a few hours."

"I trust I've satisfied *them*, at least."

Mark leaned back for the first time. "You have. But no, I never really had any uncertainties about Richard."

"At the end, neither did I. He believed he'd gotten away with two murders, so he had no reason to hesitate at a third, especially since the first two deaths were of no benefit to him if I were still alive. What other option did he have? I was dreading the ride back to Brunton. He may very well have considered it life or death to him to get me out of the way, and I told him that a moment before I ended his life."

A line from Hamlet floated through Mark's memory. *And would not let belief take hold of him, Touching this dread sight.* He had to hear every detail.

Betty stood and turned away from him. "When we left you and Kristy at the hotel bar for those few moments after your party, he went into his room to check the message light on his hotel phone at my suggestion, and I went into my room."

"To change your shoes. I didn't even notice whether you'd changed them or not later. I should have."

She faced Mark and managed a small smile. "I did change them. I wouldn't slip on such a little detail. I knocked on his connecting door, and he let me in. I confronted him with my husband's death, my son's death, and the attempt on Kristy's life." She paused to drink, and then paused some more.

"Go on," said Mark. "What did he say?"

"He denied it. Then I threw the mask at him. I told him I had found it in his apartment. I told him what Kristy and Brian said about their attacker. And then, he knew *I* knew. He asked whether I meant to turn him over to the police. That's when I took the gun from my purse."

"Where'd you get it?"

"It was my husband's."

"Where is it now?"

"After Kristy left me in her apartment the next day, I took a walk the three blocks to the Hudson River and found a secluded spot."

"You showed him the gun and then?"

"He said there was no need for a gun. He'd stay quiet while I phoned for the police. He began explaining his troubles, his gambling, his owing the wrong people money. I asked him over and over about my husband's death, but he wouldn't admit it." She paused to sip from her glass. "I guess he imagined I wasn't sure he'd done those things, so why admit anything, but he did it. I know he did it. I told him to turn onto his stomach. When he did, I shot him."

"Fortunately for you, no one heard."

"We were at the end of the hall. I'd made certain to have Richard ask for the end room, and the gun was small. I knew there would be some risk, but it was the one moment I'd planned for all along. I put the gun back into my purse, locked his connecting door, went out of his room and into mine, locked my connecting door and walked off to get the elevator."

"You had the gun in your purse the rest of the night?"

Betty nodded.

"Jesus."

Betty walked back to her chair and lowered herself slowly into it. She sat back and crossed her legs. "Now what?" she said.

"Good question."

"What are you going to do?"

"I don't know."

Betty's head dropped. "I was hoping for a friendlier answer."

"You'd like me to carry this secret to my grave."

She faced Mark again. "Yes. I don't have much of a desire to go to prison."

Mark took two slow breaths. "I don't have *any* desire to send you there. I wish now you hadn't told me."

"You saw the mask. I had to."

"You know I have no desire to harm you."

"I thank you for that," Betty said softly. "And Kristy?"

"Kristy? Are you going to tell her?"

"No," Betty said with exaggerated distinctiveness. "The question is, are you?"

"You know I won't be able to bring myself to do that."

"So?"

"So, I suppose I'll have to walk around for the next fifty years with your goddamned secret lodged in me."

"As do I."

"It isn't quite comparable."

"I know."

Mark stood. "I appreciate what you've done for me."

Betty did not respond.

Mark looked at her one last time. "I'll sit outside on the patio until Kristy gets back." He started away but stopped. "When Kristy left, she told me she hoped you were finally going to give me your blessing today. Shall I tell her that was the topic of our talk?"

"You may."

He left the house through the kitchen door.

Twenty-two

"I'm glad we're not playing for the next three days," said Kristy on Sunday night. "I felt a million miles away from the play this weekend."

"No wonder, but you did fine. I kept my eye on you."

Kristy nestled deeper into Mark's arms. They were in his bed.

"Where would you like to live?" she asked. "A new start, a clean break, would feel good right about now."

Mark kissed her lightly and stroked her cheek. "At the moment, a chateau on the far side of the moon would do. Realistically, however, anything walking distance, even a long walk, from the theater would be fine."

"Soho would be suitable, eh?"

"You have your eye on something already. I can tell."

Kristy laughed. "We're beginning to know each other too well. I do."

"Where?"

"Greene Street between Prince and Spring. A loft, but I don't know whether you want to walk up to the fourth floor."

"I walk up to the fourth floor here. I can manage as long as I'm walking up to you."

"Awwww. Sweet. And it's walking distance to the theater."

"That covers everything then."

"Do you think they'll find the person who killed Richard?" She looked up into his eyes. "Can you find out yourself? You found Ashley's and Lawrence's murderers."

Mark knew Kristy would instigate this conversation eventually, so he'd prepared his answer in advance. "Each of those murders had a story leading up to it. We know Richard's story, but this is a paid-for-hire murder. Whoever killed Richard didn't even know him. He or she left town as soon as the job ended. You see the same movies and read the same books and newspapers as I do. Moriarty's convinced that's how it happened."

"And do you really believe he killed my brother?"

"And probably your father and tried to kill you. Yes. Think about it. You can see now how desperate he must have been for money, and the higher up in your company he rose, the more he got, and probably the more he gambled. At the last, he must have known his own life was in jeopardy because of his debts, and clearly it was. So what did he have to lose by going for it all? After your mom rejected his request for a big loan that would have cleared the slate, he had no choice but to get her out of the way and gain access to the company's money, although I can't conceive how he would have gotten away with any of *that*. If he managed to, though, his troubles would have been over, at least for the moment. I suppose desperation is the mother of bad intentions."

Kristy shook her head. "I still have a very difficult time believing..." The phone rang.

"I'll get it," said Mark, glad for the interruption. He reached across Kristy for the receiver. "How are you, Detective?"

Mark could tell from Kristy's expression she hoped the call would bring news concerning Richard's murder.

"No, I don't think so," said Mark. "I'm here now with Kristy. Tomorrow would be better. Till when? Okay, but don't count on me."

Mark said goodbye and passed the receiver to Kristy, who replaced it in the cradle.

"What did he want?"

"He's alone at Phebe's and wanted to know whether I could come over for a drink."

"His wife never returned to him, I take it."

"No, no. Still off in Cold Spring 'cavorting,' as he calls it."

"It must be hard."

"He says he doesn't mind it most of the time, but obviously there are spasms of loneliness."

"Spasms?'"

"My word, not his."

"And tonight he's spasming?"

"I suppose."

"You can go over if you want to. It's not even ten o'clock yet. I'll be okay."

"He said he'd be there 'til around midnight."

"Go."

"No, I really don't want to." The last thing Mark wanted was to have an alcohol-laced, maudlin, perhaps too-penetrating conversation with a police detective. "I'd rather be here with you. Besides, I'd have to put some clothes on if I went to see him."

"True."

"I'd rather stay the way I am."

Kristy reached behind her and turned off the one light burning in the room.

"Let's go to sleep," she suggested. "Ten o'clock is late enough for us tonight, don't you think?"

"Well, we *have* expended a lot of energy since the Chinese food ran out at six-thirty."

Kristy laughed and snuggled up to him. She yawned. "I don't want to do anything these next three days except be with you."

"Suits me, darling, but I do have some theater work to do. Managing director, you know."

"I know. And some novel writing. I don't like to see you putting it off."

He glanced down at Kristy, her head on his shoulder, her eyes closed. She began to breathe rhythmically, a prelude to sleep.

Mark kissed her forehead. She smiled and sighed. Mark thought of Betty. What was she doing at this hour? Lying in bed, too, perhaps and staring into the darkness like him. Mark knew he would simply love Kristy and let everything else take its course. Contemplating Betty's crime brought a line from *Romeo and Juliet* to his mind. Romeo's father, attempting to justify to the Prince Romeo's vengeful killing of Tybalt, murderer of Romeo's friend Mercutio, says, *His fault concludes but what the law should end—*

Did Betty's fault conclude but what the law should end—the death of Richard? Maybe. Maybe not. But Romeo's dad's rationale would have to serve. He kissed Kristy's forehead again, closed his eyes, and lowered his head to meet hers.

"I love you, darling," he said softly.

"Love you, too," came back to him.

Time to rest.

Meet John Paulits

John Paulits lives in New York City and spent many years there teaching. He has written fiction for over forty years, novels for children as well as adults. *To Prove a Villain* is his fifteenth book for WingsePress. To learn more about John's books, visit him at: www.johnpaulits.com.

Other Works From The Pen Of

John Paulits

For ages 8-12

Philip Gets Even - By accident at an art show in which they are entered, Philip Felton and Emery Wyatt offend Johnny Visco, the toughest boy in sixth grade, and he promises to get even. When Johnny Visco's attacks show no sign of stopping, Philip, Emery, and Mr. Conway concoct a plan that finally puts Johnny Visco in his place and prevents him from tormenting the boys any longer.

Philip and the Case of Mistaken Identity - Philip and his best friend Emery, detectives on the trail, try to cope with a mystifying little girl who runs them a merry chase.

The Director - The Director invites nine-year-old Tommy Whitaker to be a character in a book set in 1957. The trouble begins in the Regal movie theater, where after the Saturday matinee. Elwood Wambo, the strange caretaker of the movie theater, hires Tommy and his 1957 best friend, Mouse, to stay behind on future Saturdays to clean the theater when the movie is over. The boys later learn that Wambo and his partner Jeremy are part of a gang of thieves. When their friend Smitty's bike is stolen and when Smitty himself mysteriously disappears, Tommy and his two friends, Mouse and Royal, vow to solve the mysteries of their missing friend, his missing bike...and a murder.

A Cat Tale - Hayden and his fellow cats find their way to paradise: Talula Tupperman's Home for Distressed Felines. But Rodney and Stanley, cat kidnappers, are on their trail, and suddenly cats begin to vanish. Can Hayden and his troop put a stop to these mysterious disappearances before they mysteriously vanish, too?

The Mountaintop - Jason, a seventeen-year-old Amerian, sets out for the mountaintop to determine the truth of his people's beliefs. On his journey he runs into some unexpected and eye-opening adventures. Most importantly, he meets Manda, a 17-year-old Ginder girl, who changes his life irrevocably.

For adults

Hobson's Planet - When Culp Robinson arrives on the Hobson's Planet, he steps into a whirlwind of controversy and political upheaval. Against his will, Culp finds himself the designated savior to another planet. Having failed on Earth, he wants no part of another such quest. Now he must decide where his duty and his heart lie.

Henny and Lloyd Private Eyes - Henny and Lloyd, age mid-twenties, have completed their online course in private detecting and are now licensed PIs. They've rented an office on Centre Street in downtown NYC, a rundown apartment each in Williamsburg, Brooklyn, and now set out to make their dreams of crime-fighting come true.

Ant-Nee's Golden Notebook - Mayhem and mix-ups follow Bruno Brunotaglia's murder of a hit man sent after him by a rival mob. Panic stricken, Bruno leaves behind a briefcase of money and an import notebook. Two down-and-out friends find the briefcase and notebook, and Bruno needs them back before his father, head of the Philly mob, blows a gasket. Will Richard get to keep the briefcase of money he found with Strangler and the Indian hard on his trail? Can Clarence make hay from the information in the notebook? It's a battle of half-wits in this deadly game of hide and seek.

The Sad Case of Brownie Terwilliger - Brownie Terwilliger looks at his opportunity of running for mayor of Philadelphia as a chance to right the wrongs of a city. He hopes to oust Milton Streezo, the incumbent, but Streezo does not take kindly to this challenge and concocts a plan to destroy Brownie, even hiring Lunky Ledbetter, famed perpetrator of dirty political tricks. Can Brownie withstand the onslaught? Will he have the opportunity to do some good in the world? Don't bet on it.

The Collected Short Stories - A man buried alive; the extinction of a gloried species; the mingling of interstellar races; a mysterious amulet; a fearful child; an animal-loving old hag; the assassination of the Almighty. Stories of horror, mystery, fantasy, and science fiction certain to raise the hairs on your neck.

The Rest is Silence – The Shakespeare Murders, Vol 1
When a body is found on the stage of the Bouwerie Lane Theatre, the AWB Theatre is thrown into turmoil, and Don Lovett, one of its actors, is suspected of murder. Can AWB actor Mark Louis exonerate his good friend and bring the life of the acting troupe back to normal?

A Dying Fall – The Shakespeare Murders, Vol. 2
When the AWB Theatre troupe accepts an invitation to perform on the tropical island of Illyria, they get more than they bargained for. Sudden death. The actors, however, must return home to New York, forcing company member Mark Louis to conduct his investigation a thousand miles from the crime.

Writing as Paul Johns:

From Out the Shadowed Night - How far would you go to achieve revenge? Brian Martin committed an unspeakable crime and managed to escape responsibility for his act. Now, sixteen years later, not only do the effects of his crime rise up out of the past, but something much more deadly begins to haunt him as well.

Prayer Preyer - Fifty years of obstacles have kept Jerry Curtis from locating Father Lockhart. Now, he's found the priest and is determined to take his revenge for the crime committed against him all those years ago.

Letter to Our Readers

Enjoy this book?

You can make a difference.

As an independent publisher, Wings ePress, Inc. does not have the financial clout of the large New York publishers. We can't afford large magazine spreads or subway posters to tell people about our quality books.

But we do have something much more effective and powerful than ads. We have a large base of loyal readers.

Honest reviews help bring the attention of new readers to our books.

If you enjoyed this book, we would appreciate it if you would spend a few minutes posting a review on the site where you purchased this book or on the Wings ePress, Inc. webpages at: https://wingsepress.com/

Thank You

Visit Our Website

For The Full Inventory
Of Quality Books:

Wings ePress.Inc
https://wingsepress.com/

Quality trade paperbacks and downloads
in multiple formats,
in genres ranging from light romantic comedy
to general fiction and horror.
Wings has something for every reader's taste.
Visit the website, then bookmark it.
We add new titles each month!

Wings ePress Inc.
3000 N. Rock Road
Newton, KS 67114

9 781613 095355